GHOST WORLD

Continuing their interstellar voyages, the Cosmic Crusaders find a strange planet whose inhabitants are held in thrall by a baleful hypnotic influence, reinforced by a gigantic luminescent "face" in the sky, stretching across thousands of miles of space. The servitor race are reduced to a zombie-like state, as they mine two kinds of mineral rocks, leaving them in carefully separated cairns on the surface of the planet. Periodically the rocks are collected by their alien overlords. The Golden Amazon and her fellow Crusaders soon become locked in a struggle to the death to uncover the mystery of the rock mining and overthrow a cosmic tyranny.

Another action-packed scientific adventure in the ongoing saga of the Golden Amazon!

THE GOLDEN AMAZON SAGA

GHOST WORLD

THE GOLDEN AMAZON SAGA, BOOK 19

JOHN RUSSELL FEARN

Edited by Philip Harbottle

WILDSIDE PRESS

GHOST WORLD

CONTENTS

THE GOLDEN AMAZON SERIES

by Philip Harbottle

In 1943 British writer John Russell Fearn decided to quit writing for the American pulp science fiction magazines, and to concentrate instead on books for the English market. Within a very few years he became established as a leading novelist in several genres, not only science fiction, but also mystery and detective fiction, and westerns.

His first new SF novel, *The Golden Amazon*, was published by World's Work in April 1944. In this story, a little girl of three years of age is made the subject of an idealistic scientist's illegal glandular experiments. The scientist's dream is to end world wars by creating a woman devoid of the usual lusts and frailties of mankind, who upon reaching maturity would institute a benign scientific rule. But the apparently successful experiment has a flaw: it instills into the girl a hatred for all men, and a ruthless cruelty. Her supernatural scientific gifts enable her to master atomic power, and practically leads her to destroy the world. She breaks the will and strength of men, and elevates women to positions of wealth and power. She also discovers human synthesis, and by this means she is able to escape retribution when she is eventually overthrown. She is seen to collapse and die, a victim of consuming ketabolism, echoing the memorable finale of Rider Haggard's *She*. In actuality, it was only her synthetic image, and this paved the way for the *Golden Amazon Returns*, and further sequels.

Fearn sold reprint rights in the first novel to the prestigious Canadian magazine, the Toronto *Star Weekly*. The magazine carried a special Comics Supplement, the centre section of which was a "complete novel," published in newspaper format. Aimed at a general readership, the novels were written by the top popular novelists of the day, including John Dickson Carr, Ellery Queen, and P. G. Wodehouse. They sold hundreds of thousands of copies, and the novels were syndicated to several American newspapers in the Maine and New York areas. The Amazon novels enjoyed extraordinary popularity (especially with Canadian housewives), and ran for the next sixteen years following the appearance of the first novel in the March 3, 1945 issue, ending with Fearn's sudden death in September 1960, aged only fifty-two. His final two Amazon novels appeared posthumously.

During Fearn's lifetime, only the first six novels were published in British hardcover editions from the World's Work in England, after appearing in the *Star Weekly*. This was because the publishers discontinued their entire fiction line in 1954. However, the Amazon novels continued to appear in the *Star Weekly*, eventually notching up twenty-four titles.

Fearn had resold paperback rights to the Canadian publisher Harlequin Books, but after publishing only the first three titles, they stopped publishing SF and other genre fiction to concentrate on their famous Romances line.

Meanwhile, as early as 1949, Fearn had realized that the Amazon series had the potential to run indefinitely. This presented him with a problem, however. The "origin story" of the Golden Amazon was conceived and actually set during the Second World War. Subsequent novels were written during the war and the immediate postwar period, and projected their stories only a few decades into the future.

He very astutely realized that to keep ahead of reality, he needed to move the Amazon *further* into the future—first into the outer solar system, and thence to the stars. So with the seventh novel, he introduced a new main character, Abna of Atlantis—someone equally intelligent, and even stronger than herself. These dynamics provided him with an *interstellar* canvas, thus ensuring that the series would remain ahead of reality.

Fearn's strategy was a great success, and the Amazon novels retained their popularity, ending only with his tragically early death in 1960. By then he had written a further twenty Amazon novels and made preliminary notes for his next (which would later be written by Fearn's biographer, Philip Harbottle).

Long after Fearn's death, his entire Amazon series would eventually see print from the pioneering US small press Gryphon Books in limited paperback editions, and later by the Canadian Battered Silicon Dispatch Box small press in their hardcover Omnibus series.

This new Borgo Press paperback series will be the first trade edition of all twenty-one of these later novels by Fearn, beginning with the seventh novel in the original series. First published in 1949 as *Conquest of the Amazon*, I have edited it slightly as *World Beneath Ice* (The Golden Amazon Saga, Book One) so that it can be read and enjoyed by new readers who may be totally unfamiliar with what had gone before. Subsequent novels have also been slightly edited for modern readers.

The publishers hope that this new series may create many more "fans of the Amazon." Meanwhile, any reader interested in seeking out the earlier six Golden Amazon novels will find that they are readily available on the internet, and in numerous earlier paperback and hardcover editions.

* * * *

To date, readers can enjoy the following new editions:

Book 1: *World Beneath Ice*

In destroying the threat of an alien invasion, the Golden Amazon had inadvertently caused a decline in the sun's heat, encasing Earth in an ice sheet that threatens to eliminate humanity. The Amazon encounters Abna, a descendant of Atlantis, stronger and even more scientifically advanced than she, and the ruler of an Atlantean colony still surviving in a protected environment on Jupiter. She refuses his offer of marriage, but agrees to form an alliance in order to restore the sun and save the Earth. One thing that Abna has not told the Amazon is that all the females of his race have been wiped out by a bacilli infection....

Book 2: *Lord of Atlantis*

A gigantic ridge of land rises from the Atlantic floor, causing massive tidal waves on either side of the ocean. Even stranger, both England and America are then assailed by an invasion of prehistoric monsters! A gigantic domed city rests on the newly risen plateau, whilst out in space an alien spacecraft orbits the Earth. Such are the mysteries and challenges facing the Golden Amazon, self-appointed governess of Earth, as she struggles to unravel the maze of mystery that was the deadly legacy of Atlantis!

Book 3: *Triangle of Power*

The marriage of Violet Ray Brant—better known as The Golden Amazon—and Abna of Atlantis should have ushered in an era of peace and scientific prosperity to the people of Earth. But an unexpected turn of events finds Abna betrayed and marooned on a satellite of Jupiter, and the Amazon flung far beyond the Solar System. With Earth's two protectors removed, the planet is now at the mercy of another Atlantean, the master scientist Sefner Quorne....

Book 4: *The Amethyst City*

The metaphysical union of the Amazon and Abna results in the mental creation of a fully mature daughter—Viona. Quorne, still struggling for domination, forces Viona into a marriage ceremony, and impregnates her. But with the intervention of Tarnec Brodix, a super-mind from an external universe, Quorne and Viona are separately flung into an ultra-dimensional limbo. Abna chooses to follow after his daughter, leaving the Amazon to brood over the disaster, alone in the Amethyst City of Saturn.

Book 5: *Daughter of the Amazon*

A miscalculation by the super-mathematician Tarnec Brodix destroys his universe, and the fault spreads into the Earth universe in the form of a Dark Tide of Absolute Nothingness. Unable to save himself, Brodix transfers his knowledge into the one mind powerful enough to receive it: that if Sefian, the son who has been born to Viona and Quorne. Sefian rapidly evolves, and, no longer human, after saving the Earth universe, vanishes into the greater universe, to seek new challenges. Then the Amazon is confronted with a further puzzle—a large section of the planet Neptune is discovered to be an exact duplicate of the Earth!

Book 6: *Quorne Returns*

The bacterial intelligences of Neptune plan to conquer Earth by replacing humans in key positions with alien duplicates. The Neptunians are themselves subjugated by the sinister Atlantean scientist, Sefner Quorne. Alerted to the threat, the Golden Amazon hits back by creating the ultimate doomsday weapon—only to precipitate a reprisal from the denizens of another universe....

Book 7: *The Central Intelligence*

The Golden Amazon's arch-enemy, Sefner Quorne, discovers that all mental gifts, such as memory and creativity, are something that is broadcast throughout the universe by a Central Intelligence—and then interpreted according to the quality of the individual brain of the recipient. At the surprising suggestion of his wife, Viona, the Amazon's daughter, Quorne travels with her to the very center of the universe, in order to wrest the secrets of mentality from the very source itself!

Book 8: *The Cosmic Crusaders*

The Golden Amazon renounces all ties with Earth when, together with her husband, Abna, and her daughter, Viona, she sets off on a journey to explore the cosmos. On the strange worlds of Alpha Centauri, she encounters Mizanu, the embodiment of evil—a planet-sized hypertrophied brain! Its baleful, crushing mental power threatens to reach out beyond the double-system of Alpha and Proxima Centauri to engulf the Earth and all the other inhabited planets of the galaxy—unless the Amazon can destroy it first!

Book 9: *Parasite Planet*

The Cosmic Crusaders discover a fantastic world of mental parasites drawing form and substance from our own Earth, fifty light years distant. The planet is ruled by a being identical to the Golden Amazon herself—but an Amazon who's coldly scientific and vicious, mirroring the original Amazon as she had once been early in her career. Inevitably, they become locked in a deadly duel—to the death!

Book 10: *World Out of Step*

The Cosmic Crusaders find themselves on a planet that seems mysteriously not to conform with natural law, a world out of step with the universe. It leaps ahead into time at unexpected moments, thereby suddenly adding many years of age to the flower-like inhabitants, and killing tens of thousands of individuals through death and old age. In trying to find the alien menace responsible, The Golden Amazon and her fellow Crusaders are flung backwards and forwards through time and space, threatening their own survival....

Book 11: *The Shadow People*

The Cosmic Crusaders discover a planet whose people are subject to a baleful influence from outer space that sweeps across their world—and for a brief while embraces every man, woman and child. It stirs the emotions of the sexes against each other. Men desire only to destroy women, and women men. Only those with higher types of mind are able to build a resistance against it. The struggle is dire and dreadful, and leaves its victims physical and mental wrecks. The less fortunate are left dead after the Wave has passed.

But when the Crusaders identify and destroy the source of the problem, they precipitate an even greater menace....

Book 12: *Kingpin Planet*

The Cosmic Crusaders are plunged into a strange new space, where all the probabilities of electronic law were strangely altered, a complete and stunning inversion of the so-called natural laws. They discover the mysterious silver planet of Tuca, and deep below its surface they find an enigmatic machine—the legacy of a vanished race. Masters of science, they had over-reached themselves by constructing a strange machine that could alter the very laws of nature and electronic probability. The machine had ultimately destroyed them, and blasted a neighboring planet into a cosmic cinder—and unless the Cosmic Crusaders can stop it, it may well destroy the entire universe!

Book 13: *World in Reverse*

Continuing their cosmic crusade amongst the stars, the Golden

Amazon and her companions discover a planet in another space where living beings are being synthetically created. The mystery deepens with the discovery that the synthetic race is evolving backwards! Determined to solve these mysteries, the Crusaders find themselves up against the Mithons, a sadistic alien race led by a being known as the Supreme One. Can the Amazon save the day?

Book 14: *Dwellers in Darkness*

Voyaging into a sector of interstellar space plunged into total darkness, the Cosmic Crusaders encounter a powerful and sinister mastermind, who is regarded as a God by the race he has forced to evolve without eyes. And not content with shaping the evolution of their bodies, the mastermind has also impressed on their minds an urge to conquer and dominate...

Book 15: *World in Duplicate*

In the depths of the Milky Way, the Cosmic Crusaders discover yet another mysterious planet—this time a world that appears to be a duplicate of Earth, birthplace of the Golden Amazon! Their investigations uncover a sinister plot by an alien race that threaten the Amazon's home world with complete annihilation!

Book 16: *Lords of Creation*

At first, it appeared to be a sun, forming in space where none had existed before. It kindled as an atomic fire, sustaining itself by the breakdown of fusion energies. Then, even as the Cosmic Crusaders watched, the newly-created sun was no longer just a ball of fire: it was gyrating, like a stupendous Catherine Wheel, a flaming mss spewing filaments from its edges. Then they realized the amazing truth: they were witnessing the creation of planets, flaming streamers of incandescent matter that would condense into worlds! The Golden Amazon and her fellow Crusaders grapple with the very forces of creation in their most astounding adventure to date!

Book 17: *Duel with Colossus*

From outside the universe comes a terrifying threat. A colossal spaceship materializes in the void, crewed by master scientists who have only one aim: the total destruction of the Earthly universe which, to them, is but a molecule in their macrocosm. But the invaders have reckoned without the intervention of the Cosmic Crusaders—the Golden Amazon, Abna, Viona and Mexone—who pit their strength and scientific ingenuity against Lixom, the leader of the invaders—a duel with Colossus. But it seems to be a duel that the Crusaders must lose when, separated from their mighty spaceship, the Ultra, they are projected by Lixom thousands of years into the past, to materialize—completely unprotected—in the deadly vacuum of outer space!

Book 18: *Standstill Planet*

In their latest cosmic adventure, the Golden Amazon and her fellow Cosmic Crusaders fight to save the inhabitants of the planets of an alien solar system from destruction at the hands of the Zonians. Known as "the Accursed Ones," the Zonians are attempting a monstrous super-scientific crime—nothing less than stripping their neighbor worlds of air and water. The ultimate aim is to provide this stolen air and water for an artificially created super planet. Despite the Crusaders' best efforts, two worlds are destroyed and the Zonians seem unstoppable. Can Thania, an orphaned teenage girl and the new recruit to the Cosmic Crusaders, stop their depredations?

GHOST WORLD

PREFACE

by Philip Harbottle

Ghost World was the last 'Golden Amazon' adventure to be accepted during John Russell Fearn's lifetime, and the first to appear posthumously, just three months after his sudden and premature death in September, 1960.

Fearn had submitted the mss to the Toronto *Star Weekly* editor Gwen Cowley on April 30, 1960, following an earlier exchange of letters in which she had advised the author of a reduction in the size of the *Star* novels, down from 16 tabloid pages to just 12.

When the *Star* had originally began commissioning Golden Amazon stories in 1945, Gwen Cowley had asked Fearn to submit them to a length of 45,000 words. The *Star's* editorial staff then abridged the story to a length of 40,000 words, which was the uniform length of all their "Novels of the Week". Even when the *Star* reduced its format in 1957 so that their novels had to be cut to only 31-32,000 words, they did not ask Fearn to submit the novels to a shorter length—they simply cut them further. Fearn was happy to write to the longer length, in case he had the chance to have them published in book form later.

Now, however, the situation had changed. Published lengths thereafter would be no more than 25,000 words, and the editor suggested that Fearn should submit his future mss to a length of 30,000 words; the *Star* still wished to have some 5,000 words leeway to cut and 'tighten' mss, as an aid to readability.

Fearn's covering letter read in part: 'Herewith an Amazon story tailored to 30,000 words as suggested in your letter... Am airmailing this to cut the time down and therefore have excluded the manilla cover. Hope you keep well, as we all seem to do on this side of the ocean.'

Particularly ironic (and poignant) was Fearn's inference that he was currently enjoying good health. It would therefore have came as a shock to Gwen Cowley when she received a letter dated October 6th, 1960 from Fearn's wife, Carrie Fearn:

'Dear Miss Cowley,

This is one of the most difficult letters that I have ever had to write. I have to inform you of the death of my dear husband (John Russell Fearn) on Sept 18th. He collapsed by my side in Church on Sunday morning Sept 18th and died on arrival at the hospital. He had *not* been ill at all, in fact we were looking forward to a few days holiday. I am sorry that I have not let you know before, but as you can guess the shock was so great it made me ill, so I hope you will forgive my delay. Next month (Nov 10th) we should have celebrated our fourth wedding anniversary; it seems such a short time that we have had together.

My husband had almost finished his latest Amazon story; the last few pages are in a sort of synopsis, which he would of course have filled in. I am not a writer myself so cannot do this myself, but wondered if anyone in your office would be able to do this and if so would you give it your consideration. Forgive me for asking this but it seems such a shame if my husband's last work could not be used.

I trust that all is well with you and that I may hear from you in due course.

With best wishes,
Yours sincerely,
Carrie Fearn.'

Gwen Cowley replied sympathetically and positively to the letter, and this ensuing correspondence concerning Fearn's last mss, *Earth Divided* (which it turned out *had* been completed by Fearn after all) will be highlighted in my next introduction to this final Amazon novel in the *Star Weekly* series.

Readers (including myself) of the December 17 1960 issue of the *Star Weekly* containing *Ghost World* were shocked to read the editorial note printed alongside the usual smiling photograph of the author:

Followers of the Golden Amazon and the Cosmic Crusaders adventures, will be sorry to learn that John Russell Fearn died suddenly in September. Mr. Fearn wrote countless detective and western novels and the Vargo Statten science fiction books. His Golden Amazon series, about the super-woman born during the London blitz, was created especially for the *Star Weekly*.

As a fan and reader of the novels, this news came as a terrific shock. For his widow—by his side at the time—it must have been excruciating. Her letter, written only three weeks later, shows re-markable courage, and love. It is at least some small consolation that I have been able to arrange for this latest book publication, and to dedicate it to the memory of his widow. I will write more of this remarkable lady in my next introduction.

Unfortunately, unlike the uncut versions of *Lords of Creation* and *Duel With Colossus* recently republished, no carbon of the original 30,000-word version of *Ghost World* survived, and this presented something of a problem. At only 23,000 words it was too short to run as a Borgo single novel. But I have solved the problem—and maintained uniformity with all the other books in the series—by including a "bonus" novelette to bring up the length. I am confident that all fans of the Amazon will thoroughly enjoy "Black Empress", a novelette that has hitherto never been reprinted or included in any Fearn collection. It *was* translated into Swedish (as were many of Fearn's pulp sf stories), appearing in *Jules Verne Magasinet* in 1940, but this its first English language reprint. More particularly, the character of the "Black Empress" has definite reso-nance with that of the early Golden Amazon herself. At the outset of her career the Golden Amazon was cruel and ruthless in pursuing her scientific ambitions. *"Black Empress" can therefore be read and enjoyed as a definite ancestor of the Golden Amazon,* and I feel that its inclusion here is entirely justified.

CHAPTER 1

Zombie planet

There were five people in the complicated control room of the vast spaceship Ultra. Five people—with the fabulous Golden Amazon of Earth at their head, the blonde superwoman who, with her husband Abna, had set foot upon worlds incredible beyond imagination.

The Amazon and Abna were the leaders of the band of scientific rovers known as the Cosmic Crusaders, dedicating their lives and scientific talents to the uplifting of less fortunate people on other worlds. The other members of the Crusaders were just as important in a smaller way: Viona, the daughter of the Amazon and Mexone, her husband; and of late yet another member had been added, Thania, a fair-haired teenager with mischievous gray eyes who had something in common with Viona in her love for the bizarre.

Right now they stood at the huge outlook window watching something unusual in their experience of space and its manifestations. For, what had apparently been a nebula at first sight was now increasingly revealed as a face.

"It can't be," Viona said presently, speaking the thoughts of all of them. "A face just can't be there. Why—" She turned in breathless amazement. "Think of the size of it! It must be millions of miles in area!"

The Amazon said nothing. She was staring fixedly through the window, her violet eyes puzzled.

"I've been noticing something about it," Mexone said. "It doesn't move or alter expression. Therefore it probably isn't alive, but it's the queerest thing I've ever seen."

Again silence, save for the thin, hardly distinguishable whine from the power plant. The vast machine rushed on silently through space, traveling at many tens of thousands of miles an hour. Then at length the Amazon stirred.

"Just looking out of the window and trying to guess at things isn't going to get us anywhere..." She moved actively. "What we need is analysis."

She busied herself with the switchboard. In a moment or two she had depressed relevant switches and an Analyzer came into action, a device which projected a beam ahead of the Ultra's line of flight and gave back an analysis in symbols and mathematics of whatever object it happened to strike; in this case the nebula shaped like a face.

"Well?" Abna asked, coming over to the instrument.

The Amazon indicated a display.

"X-rays in quantity," Abna said, looking over her shoulder. "And something else in high percentage—"

"The something else is platino-barium sulphide," the Amazon told him. "First time I ever heard of a nebula being composed of barium sulphide."

"Perhaps it's—" Abna started to say, but he was interrupted by an excited cry from Viona. She turned her coppery head from the window for a moment.

"Planets!" she exclaimed, jabbing a finger toward the glass. "Not far from the Face, either. They're just coming into view—or more correctly, we're just coming within sight of them."

The Amazon switched off the Analyzer, then with Abna at her side she moved back to the outlook port. There was no doubt that Viona was right. Five planets, mere pinhead specks, were now in view ahead at widely spaced distances, and they were so placed that their orbits formed an irregular circle around the mysteriously dominant face.

"That Face seems to overshadow the planets completely," Abna said, "particularly the third one away from us."

"That must be a remarkably cold system," the Amazon said. "There's no sun to warm those worlds."

Mexone said: "There's something definitely wrong somewhere. All planets shine by reflected light: They're not visible otherwise. So what makes these worlds so bright? Probably they're stars, after all."

"No, they're not stars." The Amazon shook her blonde head. "No, these are planets all right, but where they get their light from is a puzzle. Maybe we'd better study them more closely."

With that she turned to the enormous telescope and swung it around on its universal bearings until the object glass was almost in contact with the outlook port. She peered through the binocular eyepiece, adjusting it carefully until the nearest planet in the system was vividly sharp before her. She stared intently, studying a wilderness of mountains, plains, and immensely deep gorges. No sign of life anywhere.

She adjusted the telescope's focal length and, one by one, examined the surfaces of the remaining four worlds toward which the Ultra was rushing. One of the planets, the one closest to the looming Face, had distinct signs of a deserted civilization upon it—buildings, roads, parks, all arranged with obviously man-made precision, but there was no sign of a living soul. On the other hand, the outermost planet of all had civilization and life as well. There were all the evidences of people coming and going.

"Queer," the Amazon reflected, when appraisal by the others was also over. "There are five planets in the system. Three of them have apparently never been tenanted by living things. The fourth one has been populated but is now deserted, while the fifth one has a civilization of sorts, about the same as our own back on Earth. And all these worlds shine of their own accord and have no sun."

"Correct," Abna confirmed. "And on top of all that we have the Face. So what's the answer?"

The Amazon considered for a moment, then: "Most of all that Face interests me, and with the agreement of the rest of you I think we'll take a closer look at it. I suggest we cruise right into the Face and see if it's as solid as it seems to be."

Abna shrugged. "All right with me. What about you others?"

They nodded silent assent, at which the Amazon turned back to the switchboard and operated the power controls. The distant sunless system leaped sharply into new prominence and so, of course, did the enigmatic face.

"If you want my opinion," said Abna, "that face is a natural cosmic mistake—a bunch of radiations somehow coalesced together to form the outline of a face."

"There's more to it, dad, than natural formation," Viona said, "There's something mighty queer going on here and the sooner we find out what it is the better I'll—"

Quite abruptly she stopped talking, or more accurately her voice changed to a little gasp of pain as she put both hands to her face and tightly closed her eyes.

"What's the matter?" the Amazon demanded.

"I—I don't know. I felt just for a moment as though something were burning me." Viona caught her breath suddenly and stumbled away from the window. "There it is again!"

Thania said: "I—I think I can feel it, too. Not on my skin so much as in my eyes."

She covered them with her hands and staggered drunkenly away from the window. A few minutes later Mexone joined them. The only ones remaining at the window now were the Amazon and Abna, and even they could feel the strange sensation that had come upon the others.

"Radiations of some sort," Abna pronounced finally. "They come through this window because it isn't shielded from radiation to the same extent as the walls are."

"We'll soon find out what it is," the Amazon said, and hurried over to the switchboard. On the analyzing screen at the control board the answer was plain enough.

"X-rays!" Abna exclaimed. "No wonder we felt burned."

"Where are they coming from?" Viona demanded. "The Face?"

"No." There was a puzzled look on the Amazon's features. "Most of them are coming from somewhere out in space."

Risking the burning effect produced near the window, she advanced to it and looked outside.

"There!" she exclaimed, pointing as Abna joined her. "That's where they're emanating from—that planet."

Abna jumped over to the switchboard and altered the Ultra's course, sending the great vessel speeding away majestically from the leering visage in the void.

"All very interesting," the Amazon said thoughtfully. "That planet from which the x-rays are emanating is the one planet in this system which shows signs of a civilization. Yet why the inhabitants should want to create, or perpetuate, a face in infinity is a puzzle indeed."

"Perhaps," Thania hesitated, "it's some kind of god they've created."

"A good suggestion," the Amazon admitted, "but somehow I don't think it's the right one. No—that's no god. It's something much more subtle we've stumbled into. Consider the facts—the nebulous face is composed mainly of platino-barium sulphide crystals, and we have a tremendous amount of x-rays. It's an acknowledged scientific fact that x-rays excite barium sulphide."

"You're right, Vi!" Abna interrupted, snapping his fingers. "Given a field of barium sulphide crystals, as we have here, and supply the x-rays, and the field of crystals will become luminous."

The Amazon turned again to the Analyzer and switched it on.

"I just wanted to make sure," she said, switching the instrument off, "on one particular point, and I've done it. You'll be interested to know that although the x-rays are the main feature, there are also a dozen other radiations coming from that apparently civilized planet down there."

"Meaning what?" Thania questioned.

"Meaning, my dear, that there are evidently a dozen other radiations at work as 'modelers.' Radiations which are supplying their whole small contribution to the mass of x-rays, radiations which are forming eyes, nose, mouth, and little characteristics while the x-rays take on the major bulk of the job." The Amazon gave a grim smile.

"That Face could easily fool the uninitiated, but we happen lo be intelligent enough to grasp the know-how. And I'll wager that the scientists responsible are not using their talents just to prove they're artistic. They're up to something, and probably it wouldn't do any harm if we tried to find out what that something is."

"Of course," Mexone agreed promptly. "After all, that's what we're always doing, isn't it?"

"Yes, but—" The Amazon sighed. "We have to guard against being interfering, Mexone. Our job is not to barge in on unsuspecting civilizations and demand to know what they're up to—"

"That's true enough," Abna interrupted, "but it still doesn't stop us investigating. We can always move on quietly if we see no reason to suspect anything unusual or dangerous."

The Amazon smiled faintly. "I was rather hoping you'd say that. Any suggestions as to where we should begin investigating?"

It was Abna who made the decision. "I would suggest the planet that has the remains of civilization upon it."

"Why?" the Amazon questioned in surprise. "We're not going to get much out of a deserted world, are we?"

"That depends." Abna was looking thoughtful. "Sometimes the remains can show us quite a great deal, especially with the kind of instruments we carry. On the other hand, if we go to the civilized planet, we lay ourselves open to very pointed questions from the inhabitants."

"I think dad's right!" Viona exclaimed.

The Amazon said nothing, but her violet eyes glanced at the others quickly and beheld each one silently in sympathy with Viona, so without any more hesitation she turned to the switchboard and altered the controls, sending the Ultra around in a wide semi-circle and finally turning her nose toward the planet nearest the vast, looming face.

"It's manifestly impossible," Abna said, "for a system of planets like this to exist without a primary, or sun. They couldn't form orbits without a master gravitation to chain them."

"Yet there's no sign of a sun," the Amazon said.

Abna frowned. "The sun of this system could have become a dark star somehow, and would still be the center of gravity."

The Amazon turned to the control panel and switched on an instrument. After a while she switched off, and turned to Abna.

"Your guess is right. There is a dark body on the fringe of this system: This radar apparatus shows it clearly."

The planet ahead had now become wide enough to swallow up the stars. Again the Amazon turned to the control board, cut down the power, and leveled the Ultra out so that the huge vessel was flying horizontally to the disordered-looking landscape below. Lower, and lower still, losing velocity with every second, until at last the Ultra came to rest amidst a cloud of dust.

"Now," the Amazon said. "Let's see what sort of planet we've got."

She switched on the exterior analyzers and contemplated them.

"One hundred and forty degrees Fahrenheit!" Abna exclaimed over her shoulder.

"Volcanic warmth, I imagine," the Amazon answered. "But since there's a pretty low humidity reading, the conditions shouldn't prove beyond endurance."

"Oxygen 70 percent," Thania added. "That's a breathable atmosphere, isn't it?"

"Good enough," the Amazon answered briefly. "All we need are weapons and provisions."

One by one each of them turned and from lockers in the wall took prepared kits of tools, instruments and provisions. Then, the Amazon in the forefront, they stepped through the great airlock and jumped down to the surface of this new and peculiar world, which was covered with a chalk-like dust.

Somehow, everything looked unreal and photographic—the white icing-sugar buildings standing silently around them, and the enormous Face leering down at them from the sky.

"Reminds me of a graveyard," Viona said at last.

"Probably because it is one," Thania commented. "And that horrible Face! I—I just feel as though I want to run—and run—and run! Anywhere!"

She half turned as she spoke and glanced back toward the reassuring bulk of the Ultra. Then abruptly, before any of the others could grasp her intentions, she broke away from them and went speeding away through the chalky soil.

"What's the matter with her?" the Amazon demanded, her face taut.

"There's something about this place—something devilish..." Viona said, and it was obvious she was having a struggle to control herself. "I'll go and fetch her."

"You mean we all will," the Amazon said. "Come on."

She started on a swift run in pursuit of the fleeing Thania, with the others coming up quickly behind. Thania was no match for the catlike speed of the Amazon, who soon caught up with the obviously panicked girl and dragged her to a halt

"Let me go!" Thania shouted, wriggling in the Amazon's fierce clutch.

A second later the Amazon's right fist came around and hit her a resounding blow on the side of the jaw. She sagged weakly, then collapsed in the flaky dust.

"What did you do that for?" Abna demanded.

"For obvious reasons," the Amazon replied. "Something's frightened her so badly that she's on the verge of hysteria, and there's only one way to cure that. And I've done it."

After a moment's hesitation, Viona went down on her knees and gathered the limp girl's head and shoulders in her arms. She looked up at her mother.

"I'm not questioning but what you did the right thing..." she began to say, then hesitated as the Amazon cut her short.

"Thanks for your tolerance, Viona! Anything else you want to say?"

"As a matter of fact there is." Viona lifted the unconscious girl to her feet and supported her. "You ought to remember that a blow from your fist is strong enough to break the neck of a prize ox."

"Thania isn't so fragile," the Amazon said coldly. "She's had enough surgery performed on her to make her as strong as we are, so I'll wager I didn't hurt her. We can soon find out."

With that the Amazon motioned for Viona to stand aside, and she herself took the weight of the unconscious girl. She shook her fiercely, gave her little slaps in the face, and at last she began to blink into consciousness again.

"Better?" the Amazon asked briefly, and Thania nodded slowly.

"Yes—I'm better. Thanks." She gave her head a shake. "Only—"

"Only what?"

"That feeling's coming on again, somewhere inside me. A kind of mad panic. I'm terrified of something, and I don't know what it is. Can you understand it?"

"No." The Amazon's face was uncommonly set.

"Well, I can," Viona said quietly. "There's something devilish about this place. I can feel it—and so can Thania, evidently."

"Rubbish!" the Amazon said flatly.

"I don't think it is," Viona went on. "It's affecting you, too, but not in a panicky way. It's making you hard and curt instead. You're not your usual self."

"You're right there," Abna agreed anxiously.

For a moment it looked as though the Amazon was going to fly into heated rage, then evidently she got control of herself just in time.

"Yes—perhaps I have," she admitted with a frown. "I just feel that way—so much so I even enjoyed hitting Thania. I don't know why I did it."

Viona said: "You did it, mother, for the same reason that Thania bolted blindly away in an effort to escape something that isn't really there. There's something odd about this planet—something that terrorizes or unbalances the reason."

There was silence for a moment as, grim-faced, the five looked about them.

"Perhaps," Abna said at last, staring upwards, "it has something to do with that Face."

"Viona's right," Thania said suddenly, her voice taut and her gray eyes full of strain. "Something's wrong with this world, some-thing that's driven away its population. I can't stand any more of it! Let's get back to the Ultra."

"No." The Amazon shook her head. "No, we're not going to do that because that's probably the very thing we're expected to do. I've not the least doubt that we're being watched—though don't ask me from where. We won't discover anything by running away. We'll stick it, as we've always done."

"You're the boss," Abna shrugged. "But how long do you think we'll be able to hold out against this sinister influence working against us?"

"No idea. We'll stick all we can..." The Amazon gestured a trifle impatiently. "After all, there's so much to find out here. Why should people escape from this world and maintain a scarifying face and terror waves when they're the only people in this whole system? For apparently they are. All the other worlds are deserted. That face peering down from up there is being maintained for a reason, and I have the feeling that the people of this world are still here... somewhere."

There was silence for a moment; then apparently struck by a thought, the Amazon pulled an instrument from her belt and focused it up carefully. When it was to her liking, she projected the electrode end down toward the ground and read the reactionary needle on the dial.

"That explains why everything's so light," she said, indicating it. "There's a very high proportion of radioactive mineral in this planet."

She began moving through the ashy dust, picking her way over boulders and collapsed girders, looking about as she went. The others followed.

As they advanced they fought continually against the terror-waves. To the Amazon and Abna, with their highly balanced and resistant minds, it was not so much a struggle as a flat, uncompromising refusal to be broken down by anything alien to their own desires.

After a while Abna called a halt. "Better not go too far," he cautioned. "We don't want to get out of touch with the Ultra."

They looked back towards it but could not see it. The place where it had been was nothing but an amphitheatre of gray dust.

"Where's—where's it gone?" Viona asked uncertainly.

For answer the grim-faced Abna pulled an instrument out of his belt and snapped on the activating button. He spoke as he worked. "To the eye the Ultra has completely vanished— Ah!" He broke off suddenly, with obvious relief. "It's still there. There's a distinct reaction from the Ultra's magnetic prow. Look at the needle here."

The others looked at the undeniable evidence

"The Ultra is covered in dust," the Amazon explained, "and therefore looks like one of the many small hills scattered about this region." Her hand pointed. "I'd say that's it."

The others gazed at one distant hill in particular, its base marked by what appeared to be a cave.

Then the Amazon spoke again. "The hole at the bottom isn't a cave: it's the airlock. Naturally the magnetism of the ship has drawn the metallic dust to itself and given it an overcoat."

The Amazon would probably have said more but Thania clapped both hands to her head and gave a piercing scream. Then without explaining herself she dashed away at a stumbling run.

Viona followed in pursuit but before she had gone a dozen yards there was a wild, panic-stricken cry from the teenager and she suddenly disappeared into the ground. The others blinked, and Viona in particular. Then she was on her way again, stumbling over the broken stones and girders until she came to a jagged hole in the ground not six yards away. When she found that the ground was no longer firm, she got down on her knees and gently crawled to the edge of the hole to have a look.

She could not quite believe what she saw. She was looking down at a city. Or was it a city? All she could make out were thousands of luminous dots—completely immovable—just like the lights of a city at night.

"Thania?" she called at last. "Thania, are you there?"

"Here!" came the faint response. "I'm on a sort of ledge."

Viona reached back with difficulty into her belt and tugged out a high-power atomic torch, which she shone into the space below. Almost immediately she saw Thania lying sprawled face upwards on a jutting finger of rock.

"Use your own torch to show your position," Viona instructed, "then I'll come and get you."

"I—I can't. My back won't bend. I'm…hurt."

"Hang on," Viona called, switching off. "I'll be with you in a moment."

She glanced up as, with delicate steps the Amazon, Abna and Mexone reached her side. As quickly as she could, Viona explained the position.

"I'd better go," Abna said, uncoiling a length of tough nylon rope from his belt.

He gave the rope to the Amazon, and she tied it around her slim waist, then braced herself for the strain. Abna lowered himself into the hole, eased himself down, then let himself go.

All he could see at first were mineral-veined rocks, some of them glowing with odd phosphorescence. Then he came in sight of the jagged ledge on which Thania was sprawled. He released the rope suddenly and plunged the last few feet to hard rock. In a matter of moments he was at her side.

"My back," Thania whispered. "I—I can't move it or bend it."

"Just lie still," Abna murmured as he took her into his arms. "Maybe a little metaphysical process can put things right."

Thania had never before experienced the metaphysical power of

Abna—a power that he alone of all the party possessed—and now that she did begin to feel it, it was a wondrous and blessed thing. As moments of silence continued, as Abna held her with a gentle but rigid tightness, she felt the grinding pain and stiffness ease from her body. Finally she opened her eyes.

"Better?" Abna asked gently.

"It's more than that. It's gone altogether... Oh, Abna, what a wonderful man you are!"

"I'm not a wonderful man, really, you know. I'm a rather hard-bitten, seven-foot tall adventurer from Jupiter. What powers I have are natural gifts, so there's nothing really wonderful about them... Now—" His powerful hands gripped her. "Let's see how you can stand up."

In a moment Thania was on her feet.

"As good as new!" she exclaimed.

Suddenly there was a blaze of light from above, accompanied by the voice of the Amazon. "What's going on down there? Is everything all right, Abna?"

"Everything's just fine," he replied. "Thania's just—" He broke off abruptly and turned as Thania clutched tightly at his arm. He sensed the urgency in her grip, and in another moment understood why. Somebody, or something, was approaching up an acclivity in the distance.

"People of some sort," Thania whispered. "We're right in their path, too. What do we do?"

Abna called sharply above. "Put out your light, Vi. There's some kind of life down here. I'll contact you later."

The torchlight expired. Abna and Thania stood close together, watching the distant rocky slope along which lights were moving—lights that were presumably carried by people.

The two Crusaders moved quickly and silently behind a tall rock spur. Presently a file of about 20 men and women, scantily clad, and looking exactly like Earth people in appearance, each one bearing an electric light on their heads fitted to some kind of coronet fixture, came into view on the ledge from the acclivity.

They looked neither to right nor to left. As they came nearer, Abna and Thania could see they were each carrying two pieces of rock, one on each shoulder.

"They move as though they're sleep-walking or something," Abna murmured.

"Like zombies," the girl muttered.

Each of them had a deadpan, expressionless face with eyes staring straight in front. When the last one had gone by, Abna scrambled to his feet.

"I'm following them to see where they go," he said. "You get back up above to safety. The rope's still hanging."

He slipped away into the gloom in pursuit of the bobbing lights. Thania turned and saw something—a zombie coming toward her with a rock load, a lamp blazing brightly on his head.

Sheer panic gripped her as he came steadily on. In a matter of moments he was upon her and finding her blocking his path, he set down the two rocks he was carrying. Without speaking he gripped her around the waist and threw her away from him. Helplessly she collapsed amidst dust and rock chippings. Then she suddenly remembered the protonic gun in her belt.

But before she could level the weapon, the zombie dived upon her and, snatching the gun from her hand, twisted her arm backwards and upwards. Thania screamed with the pain of it, but the creature held on with relentless clutch, his other hand seeking for her throat. Suddenly he found it and gripped with a clutch of steel.

Thania squirmed helplessly. She felt herself growing weaker as, through a blur, she saw a figure apparently drop from the skies.

"Amazon—" Thania managed to croak. Then her senses gave out just as the zombie was torn from her by the Amazon's steel-strong hand.

The zombie turned at the new visitation and simultaneously a fist slammed straight into his face with shattering power. It was a blow that would have nearly killed an ordinary being, but in this instance it hardly had any effect, and the Amazon was left gritting her teeth at the pain in her fingers.

But in trying to defend himself, the zombie exposed himself to the Amazon's favorite killer-blow. As her fist crashed into his neck, he collapsed to the dusty floor with his nerve centers paralyzed.

The Amazon turned to the slowly recovering Thania and hauled her to her feet.

"Where's Abna?" she asked the girl.

"He's following a crowd of these zombies somewhere."

They glanced up as there were sounds of movement above. Mexone and then Viona came sliding down the nylon rope into the underworld.

"What's going on?" Mexone asked, and at that the Amazon indicated the zombie stretched in the dust. She told them about the attack on Thania.

"Is he dead?" Viona asked.

The Amazon shook her head. "Anything but, I imagine. These people are the toughest I've ever encountered. I would have killed him straight off with my gun, but I wanted to keep him for the purpose of learning what kind of a set-up really operates on this world."

She broke off as a sound caught her attention in the distant gloom. Then the giant figure of Abna came into view. They brought him up to date on events, and then asked him where the zombies had gone.

"To the surface, and that's about all I can tell you. They went to a kind of natural ramp that leads up out of the underworld, but after that… Well, I just don't know." Abna sighed and rubbed the back of his head in perplexity. "Each man and woman put down his or her donation of rock in a neat cairn, and then dashed for the safety of the underworld as though demons were after them. I don't grasp the point at all—all the left-hand shoulder rocks in one place and the right-hand shoulder rocks in another. Just left there! It doesn't make sense."

"Since you saw the people dash back into the underworld," the Amazon remarked, "we'll be seeing them here again soon, won't we?"

"As a matter of fact, no." Abna shook his head. "Once they came back into the underworld they went down a declivity and that was the last I saw of them. It seems evident that they have one way to come and another to go. Where are the rocks this fellow was carrying?"

The Amazon pointed them out to him, but Abna found nothing significant about them. He finally tossed them away over the edge of a rimrock in disgust, and in that moment astounding things happened.

The instant the rocks struck the ground—one on top of the other as it happened—there was a flash of intensely blue, unbearable light, followed instantly by a shattering explosion. It was an explosion out of all proportion to the size of the rocks.

The Crusaders were instantly thrown down. Gradually the violent disturbance ceased and a fine fog of white dust settled over everything.

"What in cosmos was that?" the Amazon demanded as she got to her feet. "It went off like a nuclear bomb!"

Puzzled, their heads still singing, they all moved to the spot where the rocks had been thrown. It lay just over a dip in the rimrock—on the acclivity itself but the surprising thing was that the upward slope in the rocks had vanished. Instead there was an enormous, gaping hole from which sulphuric-smelling smoke was discharging.

Finally the Amazon said: "Either the rocks somehow detonated volcanic gas by friction on impact or—"

"Or," Abna finished for her, "the two rocks struck against each other as I threw them, and produced the explosion."

"But how could that happen?" Viona demanded.

Abna smiled grimly. "It's possible, if the constitution of the rocks is so arranged that it can bring it about. Remember they're mainly radio-active and not normal rock. Yes," Abna went on, thinking, "I believe it's the answer. It explains why the zombies are at such pains to keep the rocks separate from each other; why they place them in two distinct piles once they reach the surface."

"It solves one point and makes another," the Amazon commented. "It deepens the mystery as to why. What kind of fantastic beings are these that they'll risk instant death stumbling up a rubbly slope with a deadly rock on each shoulder? Why, one slip might bring the rocks, together and blow them to eternity—" The Amazon stopped abruptly as she detected a movement nearby.

"The zombie I knocked out!" she exclaimed. "He's recovering."

She darted forward and dragged the still dazed man from the debris. He stood up and just looked, making no effort this time to show fight.

"I want to talk to you," the Amazon said grimly, facing him. "Can you understand me?"

There was no response. The dull eyes in the deadpan face just gazed fixedly in front.

"We'll take him back to the Ultra and find out with our apparatus what's the matter with him," Abna said.

CHAPTER 2

Crusaders enslaved

Back in the Ultra, the Amazon switched on one of the machines and a pale yellow beam enveloped the zombie from head to foot. On the machine's dial a needle flickered over a variety of symbols, which, in their entirety, gave an analysis. The Amazon wrote down the various findings, and then handed her sheet of calculations to Abna.

"From this," he said to the others, "it would seem that our friend is fully and completely alive, despite his queer appearance. He also has all his own individuality, but it is swamped by a greater power taking control—which is something I can well believe."

He was silent for a moment, reading further, then: "So that's why he's so tough! Every cell of his body has been hardened to three times normal." He put the paper down. "Well, what do you suggest we do now?"

"The only thing," the Amazon responded. "Try to learn something from him."

"How?" Viona questioned. "His mind's obviously dominated by something else. How do you propose breaking through the barrier?"

"With one of our thought amplifiers," the Amazon said, pulling the instrument in question forward on its rubber wheels. "It's possible that ordinary thought waves won't penetrate the fog around this creature's brain, but when they're amplified there might be success."

"I'll handle the Language Translator," Viona said quickly, attaching sucker-like electrodes to the man's head. His language—both spoken and written—was absorbed into the amazing machine as his mind was read, and then re-interpreted into English. The task completed, Viona added: "If our deadpan friend is moved to speak in his own language, the translation can be made for us, and vice-versa."

So a task was begun which, in all, occupied all of two hours. During that time the mental resistance of the zombie was broken down, and he decided to talk, in a shrill and incomprehensible language. Immediately the electronic translator took up the task of translation and transmitted a normal but mechanical voice through its loudspeaker.

"I can hear all you say, strangers, and while this mental freedom lasts I will try to answer your questions, even though I do not know who you are. I have no name—only a number, and that in your mathematics I would place as 46."

"Are you a slave?"' the Amazon demanded. "Is that why you have no name and only a number?"

"That is why I, and thousands like me, were born into slavery and have been dominated ever since. It is the Face—the Face in the Heavens. That has made us slaves."

"What is the purpose of this slavery? What are you doing?" the Amazon questioned.

"We have not been told that. For generations this domination has gone on. Our ancestors fought against it, but were beaten. They had to obey the commands given them, even though to escape the Face, which gives the commands, they fled into the underworld of this planet, leaving their civilization—which has since crumbled into ruins... But even in the underworld we were not safe. The commands reached us even there and gradually, we have succumbed to them so that now we do nothing but obey. All we have in our minds is to mine two mineral substances in shifts, day and night. The two minerals are never to be in contact with each other, and are to be carried endlessly to the surface world and left at a certain place. They are to be carried always by a slave and not entrusted to any mechanical system capable of causing any jarring."

"And when these minerals have been taken to the surface and left there, what happens?" the Amazon demanded.

"I do not know. Few of us do; but there are rumors of beings who come and take the mineral loads away. I have never seen it done.

The Face is too terrifying to endure when we are on the surface."

The Amazon reflected, then said: "A little while ago you attacked and nearly killed this girl here." She nodded to Thania. "Why?"

"I merely follow orders, namely to destroy anybody or anything which hinders our journey to the surface when we are carrying a load. Then we—"

Quite suddenly No. 46 stopped talking and, of course, the translator stopped, too. He made a queer, strangling noise in his throat, seemed to shudder for a moment, and then his head dropped weakly to his chest. The Amazon felt his pulse, and then turned to the others.

"Dead," she announced.

Abna said grimly: "For all we know, the powers back of all this jiggery pokery may have a system of radio pick-ups by which they can hear what the slaves are up to. They could have heard 46's revelations and using remote mental control wiped him out before he could tell too much. They appear to have switched off his entire nervous system! You agree Vi?"

"Which means," the Amazon answered, "that the Ultra's not so proof against radiations and waves as we imagined—or at least the forces being used here." She was about to continue, but hesitated and raised a hand for silence. Almost immediately the others became aware of what had become apparent to her ultra-sensitive hearing... A thin whining sound from somewhere outside, growing ever louder. They dashed to the airlock and peered outside.

Something was sweeping down from the upper heights of the sky—a huge 'S' of fire.

"Spaceships!" Viona exclaimed.

"What do we do?" Mexone demanded urgently.

"They can't have seen us yet; they're too far away," the Amazon replied. "The Ultra's hidden, too, thanks to this dust being everywhere. I suggest we go outside, keep ourselves hidden by the city ruins somehow, and then watch what happens."

As quickly as possible the five Crusaders hurried toward the nearest mass of twisted metal and masonry. Once under cover they watched ship after ship come sweeping down. When they had landed there were about a dozen all told.

Presently a group emerged from the ships. The beings moved with a certain air of military precision, consistent with their wearing of identical tunics.

They marched promptly to the huge cairns of rock which had been placed in position by the zombies. Then, with a tremendous and exaggerated caution, they each shouldered a piece of rock and carried it back to one of the spaceships.

This continued for a while, and then the men suddenly stopped their work and headed at a run straight for the ruins where the Crusaders were hiding.

Gun in hand, the Amazon leaped from her hiding place to meet the rush of men half way. With the other Crusaders following, she fired ruthlessly at the advancing file.

In all directions men fell and vanished, but the remainder still came on, and in the end the Crusaders found themselves in the dust, chains clamped around their wrists and ankles.

A commanding officer approached the prisoners. He was a tall man, with an air of haughty intolerance. So similar was he to an Earthman in physique—at least outwardly—it was difficult to realize he was a denizen of a far-flung world in the First Galaxy.

A short, vicious-tailed whip lay in one of his six-fingered hands. He beat it gently in the palm of his other hand, and smiled.

"I had expected something more subtle from the Cosmic Crusaders," he commented in English. "That was very crude, besides being costly to my men. It also placed all of you in considerable danger but, as you must have noticed, we did not attempt to kill you as you did us."

The Amazon stared malevolently, her purple eyes glinting.

"And now," the commander said, smiling again, "you're wondering who I am and why I speak your own tongue so fluently. My name is Agos Thar, and I'm the military commander of my planet and also the adviser to its scientific government. As to your language… Well, since you arrived in this system you have talked a lot."

"What's that got to do with it?" the Amazon snapped.

"I'll tell you. Our language translation machines have analyzed your speech and actions and worked out your language, in which myself and a few of my closest aides have been instructed. We—that is, the people of my planet—are all blessed with photographic brains. Whatever we hear or see we never forget. It was only necessary for us to hear your language once to have the mastery of it."

"You say you've been hearing our voices," Abna said. "By remote radio techniques, I presume?"

"Exactly. Quite naturally, you're wondering what is happening on this planet—why the people are slaves and carry rocks. Since, as I think, you know already that contact of two of the rocks produces a devastating energy, I may as well explain the rest of it. It won't do you any good even when you know our purpose..."

He slapped the butt of his whip in his palm and then continued. "We have in mind nothing less than the rekindling of our sun, which through a cosmic cloud was reduced to a dead star many centuries ago. This disaster is the greatest mystery in our history—some of our scientists have conjectured that it was not a normal cosmic accident, but may have been engineered by some malign alien race from the stars. They may have used our solar system as some kind of experimental laboratory to test their ultimate weapon—a sun killer—before moving on to attack their enemies in some other system. Not that it signifies...

"Once our sun is rekindled, our system can again live to the full in overhead light and warmth, and will not have to rely on radioactive and volcanic power to be assured of a means of existence."

"We have already detected a dead star in this system," the Amazon said. "That, I suppose, is your one-time sun?"

"That is correct. But, since you yourselves are scientists, consider the intricacies involved. First, the rocks of this world have to be transported to the dead star, a process that has already been going on for many years. Secondly, when they have been transported, there remains the very dangerous and exacting task of bringing two rocks of the opposing values into contact in close proximity to the remainder of the rocks. That will be done by machines, of course, but in control of the machines there must be intelligent beings whom we can implicitly trust. Once the moment of rock contact is gained there will be no stepping back. The explosion of one rock pile will trigger the next, and the effect will spread almost simultaneously. The instant fusion of a sun's core will take place, and in that inconceivable fury of atomic energies, those who have started the celestial holocaust must surely perish. There will not be time for them to escape."

Agos Thar paused and glowered down on the five adventurers sprawled around him. "Do I make myself clear, my friends?"

"Not entirely," Mexone remarked, frowning. "You say you have been transporting rocks to the surface of your dead sun. How is such a thing even possible? The tremendous solar heat may be absent, but surely the tremendous solar *gravity* must remain? Any spaceship and its crew trying to land on the surface of a star would be instantly crushed and smeared by the gravity..."

"That's right," Viona put in. "When we entered this system we discovered that its planets were revolving around this dead sun as the center of gravity."

Argos Thar gave a contemptuous smile. "Certainly our sun's gravity affects the planets," he conceded, "but that effect only obtains at a distance from our primary. But nearer to it, and on its surface, the effect of gravity is greatly nullified. The energies used by our ancient violators, which impregnated and destroyed the atomic processes of our sun, created a side-effect of neutralizing and reducing the surface gravity to that of a medium-sized planet. No doubt this was to enable the aliens to descend and examine its surface to view the results of their experiment. Fortunately for us, this effect is still in operation."

"But if your sun now has only planetary gravity," Mexone persisted, "how can its influence extend to all of the planets in this system?"

"I think I know the answer to that one," Abna said, thinking. "Gravity is not an actual force as such, remember. It is a curvature in space-time, caused by mass-weight. Away from its surface, the sun's gravity still has the same effect on the space surrounding it."

"Very clever of you," Argos Thar remarked, his contemptuous smile returning. He looked at the others. "So now do you understand?"

"Entirely," the Amazon answered grimly. "You are implying that the five of us here are just the people for the task you have in mind."

"Precisely..." Agos Thar spread his hands and was smiling

again.

"And if we had not chanced to come here, what would you have done?" Abna demanded.

"In that event, slaves from this world would have been used, but since every slave on this planet is useful, whereas you five are unwelcome visitors, it is obvious to me that in dying you should prove yourself useful."

"And you think we'll obey your orders?" Viona demanded.

Thar said coldly: "I'm sure you will. In fact, you won't be in any fit state to do otherwise by the time we have finished with you... You must have noticed, since arriving here, the atmosphere of intense compulsion that pervades this place? An atmosphere which saps the individual will and makes it amenable to the orders of another?"

"Yes, we've noticed," the Amazon confirmed. "Presumably waves of radiation from your planet designed for the special purpose of dominating the people of this world."

"Yes, that is the situation," Thar agreed. "The only impedance in our plan has been the arrival of yourselves, but as I have said, we shall turn that impedance to good account even as you destroy yourselves."

Abna said curtly: "Don't be too sure of yourself, my friend. Our scientific knowledge is easily level, and probably in advance, of yours."

"I agree entirely," Thar said. "Which is something I intend to take care of right away. I know that the mental compulsion and terror waves from my planet affect you very strongly—against which all of my race, including myself, have complete immunity due to our physical design. So, since you are affected, it must be made absolute, until in the end you are just living-dead tools of our will. In that state you'll carry out our orders to rekindle our dead sun."

Silence greeted Agos Thar's pronouncement. Then suddenly something happened.

The Amazon's arms, which had been pinioned behind her back with chain, suddenly whipped forward to the accompaniment of a click as links broke. All the time she had been talking or listening to Thar she had been silently at work on the links. Her hands shot forward and grasped both Agos Thar's ankles. Quite unprepared for the maneuver, he staggered and then crashed over on his back.

Instantly the Amazon heaved herself up and her hands closed relentlessly around Thar's neck.

The assembled men moved indecisively, groping for their guns, until at length the Amazon checked them.

"Better not," she advised, trusting they would understand the language. "One bad move on the part of any of you and it's the end of Agos Thar! That's just a warning."

The men hesitated, then turned their attention to Thar as he managed to gasp out a few words.

"Do as she tells you, whatever it may be. She is not the kind of woman to make idle threats."

"Very sensible of you." The Amazon gave a hard grin and still kept her hold on Thar, who had now ceased to struggle. "All right, release us, and then I'll tell you what comes next."

Within a minute all five were completely free, but still without their guns. The Amazon retained her hold on Agos Thar.

"Get some guns, Abna!" she ordered.

Abna nodded promptly, and glanced at the nearest guard, but before he could move the unexpected happened. Agos Thar heaved upwards viciously. The Amazon, her hold but slightly relaxed for a moment, lost her grip and went reeling sideways. She was on her face in the ashy dust before she knew what had happened, and simultaneously Abna and the others found themselves set upon and battered unmercifully with gun butts.

Only for a moment was the Amazon incapacitated, then her quick brain reacted. Even as Thar's hand came down toward her, she shot out her right arm and gripped his wrist. He screamed under the awful pressure as the wrist bone snapped, but it was a scream abruptly cut off as the Amazon lashed up her right foot and kicked him straight in the face.

He reeled back, blood streaming from his cut nose and lip.

Suddenly a gun was jammed in the small of the Amazon's back.

"Better not!" one of the guards said coldly, in awkward English.

The Amazon lowered her arm and waited.

With an effort, Agos Thar got to his feet. Retrieving his whip with his good hand, he shook out the twin fine metal tails, his vicious eyes on the Amazon's coldly beautiful face. He lashed the whip downwards with demoniacal force, only just missing the Amazon's right eye as he struck her on the face. She tensed for a moment with the pain, then slowly fingered the deep cut which was already starting to bleed.

"Just a slight repayment," Thar explained bitterly, dabbing at his face.

"Some day," the Amazon said slowly, her voice perfectly level, "you'll answer for that whip cut, Agos Thar."

Thar signaled to his men with his sound arm. "Chain them up again."

The guards obeyed, and the Crusaders were shoved violently over on to their backs.

At Agos Thar's orders, several of the men got shovels from their space machines and began to dig up the soil until they had five narrow, crudely made pits.

"I have decided to subdue you," Thar commented. "You are far too fractious at the moment."

Again he signaled and this time, one by one, the five were dragged to their feet, hauled over to the holes in the ground, and dropped into them. Then the ashy soil was shoveled in around them till they were packed tight up to their chins.

"Comfortable?" Agos Thar asked cynically.

"Just what do you hope to gain by this?" the Amazon demanded.

Thar smiled. "I intend to use all five of you as I have said, but by the time I am ready for you I want all your individuality to be destroyed. Which it will be, after this. My colleagues and I have a journey to make to our dead star with the rock we have collected. You will stay where you are until we return, exposed to the radiations, which do not affect us but which, we realize, have disastrous effects on your particular constitutions."

The Amazon said: "I have already warned you that one day I shall repay you, Agos Thar, and nothing you have done, or are going to do, can change my decision."

Thar shrugged. "You might die, Amazon—all of you might. Die from madness and hunger and thirst. A vicious combination for all of you to combat, you must agree."

The Amazon did not reply. She closed her eyes as Thar drew back his foot to deliver a smashing kick at her head; but the vicious expected blow did not fall. Instead he smiled.

Then suddenly swinging around, he motioned to his men and led the way back to the space machines. One by one the airlocks closed and the machines took off.

"Well, can't you do something?" Thania demanded, with a touch of hysteria.

"Take it easy!" Viona ordered curtly. "You're the only one, dad, who can help us."

"I?" Abna turned his head.

"Well, this is plainly a matter for metaphysics."

"Sorry; I can't." Abna shook his blond head almost ferociously. "There's too much mental disturbance for me to get the required poise necessary."

Nobody said anything. It was just beginning to dawn on them that this was one trick the sadistic Agos Thar had definitely won. And with every moment the sinister waves generated from the 'civilized' planet were making their presence felt more and more.

Minutes passed as all five wrestled for an answer. But there just wasn't one, or if there was, they could not discipline their minds enough to think of it. And because their minds were extraordinarily sensitive and receptive, the more rapid was the deterioration as the waves of disorder, fear and unreasoning hatred crept into their conceptions.

Suddenly there was one of those dust eddies which seemed inseparable from this world. Ashy dust blew in the Crusaders' faces, setting them blinking furiously. In the Amazon's case, the dust grains stuck to the drying blood on her cut face and created appalling irritation—but there was nothing she could do about it.

Then finally, as the miniature whirlwind subsided, Thania let out a scream of protest. "Do something, can't you! We can't put up with this kind of misery any longer."

The others did not answer, knowing as they did that they were completely helpless to aid her. They watched in anxious sympathy as Thania struggled madly to free herself, but with all her efforts, forced finally to frenzy by the relentless waves beating down on her, she could not budge a fraction of an inch. So finally she relaxed weakly, her head lolling. She seemed hardly alive any more.

So it went on, minute after minute, hour by hour, with only an occasional dust storm to relieve the monotony. Once and once only the zombies came up from below with a load of rockery, and having once deposited it, they returned to the underworld without looking either right or left.

Not that the Crusaders cared any more. Their minds did not seem to be their own any more: They kept on repeating constantly the mental commands that were being dinned at them. There were many of them—too many to differentiate—but the main theme seemed to be to obey, so this they were prepared to do if it mean any relief from their torture.

Finally all five Crusaders closed their eyes and relapsed into something that was close to coma. The next conscious thing they knew was that Agos Thar had returned, his broken wrist and damaged face now apparently restored. One by one, each Crusader was hauled up bodily.

Only then did Thar speak. "From the look of you, Amazon, I would say that much has been accomplished during our absence. Fourteen hours of soaking in the compulsion waves, plus the absence of food and drink, has made your minds and bodies completely subservient to us, which is as I intended."

The Amazon did not answer. She was trying hard to get control over herself, to get life into her numbed body. Her dull eyes turned as one of the guards gave a sharp exclamation.

"Commander, quickly! Come and look!"

Thar obeyed, hurrying over to the guard who was holding the slack, unchained figure of Thania in his grip. There was something about her attitude which made momentary reason return to the Amazon's mind. She and the others watched as Thar quickly examined the girl, then he jerked his shoulders in an obviously negative action and dumped her back in the hole from which she had been dragged.

"What's wrong with her?" The Amazon found it extremely hard to talk coherently.

"Dead, if you must know." Thar's voice was laconic. "Evidently not as tough as the rest of you. There are no heartbeats."

"Thania…dead?" Abna repeated. He wanted to fell Agos Thar to the ground there and then, but somehow he had not the initiative or the strength.

"That's what I said," Thar confirmed. "Now, move, all of you! To the nearest spaceship."

The four Crusaders did not attempt to argue: They passively obeyed and began to walk with the familiar, slouching step of the underworld zombies, doing exactly what Agos Thar had ordered.

Once only did they glance back at the dead face of the teenage girl who had wanted to taste the thrill of life on distant worlds… and found death.

The rest was mechanical. They entered the big control room of the nearest ship, but took no interest in their surroundings or the equipment, so dulled and over-mastered were their brains. They were given a meal when the vessel got under way into space, but although the food and drink certainly restored their strength, it did nothing to bring their minds back to normal. The Amazon, Abna, Viona and Mexone were no longer superbeings—except in muscular power. They were zombies like those in the ghost underworld, complete slaves of the radiations pouring forth from Agos Thar's world.

The journey through space to the dead sun was not a vastly long one, it seemed. Or maybe it appeared that way to the Crusaders since they were no longer able somehow to assess time or distance. They only knew that through the period they sat and waited—and once even slept—a fair distance must have been covered for the vast dead star was now plainly visible through the observation window.

CHAPTER 3

Free from compulsion

Silent on their bunks, the four Crusaders sat gazing dully on the dark, somber mass of what had once been a flaming sun. Agos Thar came in from his own quarters in another part of the space machine. He looked briefly through the window and then turned to the Crusaders.

"You should feel honored, my friends," he remarked cynically. "To you falls the privilege of restoring a sun to our cold and lightless system. Come to the window and see how much has been done already."

The quartet rose and looked more closely on the huge dark area being circled at about 5,000 feet. They simply saw, and that was all. There was no sharp mental picture in their minds, no keen analysis of the situation.

The view was that of an immense dark plain, picked out at various intervals by areas of white, which looked like mountains at this height. The four struggled in their minds to realize what the white areas meant. Then Agos Thar explained for them.

"You are looking, my friends, on the millions of square miles of radioactive rock which have been brought here through the centuries by myself and my predecessors. A vast and necessary work indeed! Observe that each mountain range, which is really stacked-up rocks, is connected to the next one by a line of more rocks. In fact, this whole solar surface is covered, awaiting the supreme moment when the ignition shall take place. Then indeed all this will fuse, ignite, and continue to blaze and emit energy for centuries untold."

The quartet just stared at him, and that was all. He looked at their faces for a moment, then with a gesture of irritation, motioned them back to the bunks. The four turned mechanically, walked back across the control room and sat down.

"For the moment," Thar said, coming over to them, "that is all I have to show you. I know it has penetrated your brains even though there is no visible reaction. Until the time when you are to make the actual journey—the course and direction of which is now engraved in your minds for future use—you will work as the others. Regrettable perhaps to fall so completely from your scientific eminence, but it has to be."

No answer. The quartet on the bunks were too busy with their own mental troubles to listen to Thar. The only thing that had really registered on them was his statement to the effect that they knew now all the details of the journey they would eventually make. This was correct, and had evidently been the main purpose of the trip. Photographically, in some odd way, they knew exactly what they would have to do—but everything else was still blurred and somehow unreal.

"Once we return to the slave planet there is a special detail I must attend to…the matter of your spaceship."

At that, something penetrated the fog in the Amazon's mind. She looked up sharply, her main thought being that the Ultra was the only link with safety.

"What—what about our spaceship?" she questioned, with a curious uncertainty of speech.

"So that stirs your brain to life, does it?" Thar asked dryly. "You ask what about it… I will tell you. I intend to destroy it. You probably entertain the odd notion that I don't know where it is, but I do. Buried in ash-dust on the central plain. Don't forget that telescopic eyes watched you and your machine from the moment you first entered this system. Uninvited, I would add. So, obviously, the machine must be destroyed, even as you must be in the end."

The faint restoration of intelligence which the Amazon had experienced died again and she sat in dumb silence as Thar finished speaking, a silence which also gripped Abna, Viona and Mexone. Though they knew what Thar intended doing, though they knew that the destruction of the Ultra would banish forever all their hopes of escape, they did nothing to avert it. Indeed they could not. The power of individual reason was suspended—whether permanently or temporarily they could not tell.

The return to the slave planet was soon completed, the quartet passing some of the time in a curious kind of drugged sleep, which was a condition usually foreign to them. They awakened from the last of these sleeps to the realization that the vessel had landed back on the ashy plain from which it had started, the only change being that the other space machines which had been present had now disappeared, presumably to their own world.

"It occurs to me," Agos Thar said, surveying the scene outside through the observation window, "that this might be an excellent opportunity for you, my friends, to study the outcome of a fusion of these radioactive rocks. I know you have already seen, by accident, the power of them, but maybe a first-hand view will be more impressive."

His words sank in but produced no reaction. He turned to his crew of men and singled out two of them. He spoke a few words in his own language to them, then opened the airlock, and they stepped outside.

The two guards came into view through the observation window, each carrying a chunk of rock on his shoulder.

"You should find this interesting, my friends," Thar said. "My men are going to deal with your spaceship, under the dust hill out there. Watch carefully."

The quartet did so, looking but not observing.

One of the men burrowed into the ground in front of the ashy gray hill under which the Ultra lay hidden; then the second man began to weigh and test the weight of the rock he was carrying.

"Unfortunate perhaps that our two friends outside are going to meet certain death," Thar commented with brutal frankness. "However they know the glory of dying for a cause... Here, put these on."

The Crusaders found dark goggles being dangled before them. They put them on and then gazed at the plain outside.

"I think we're ready now," Thar commented, and through the goggles the remaining man carrying the piece of rock could be seen hurling it forward. The moment it left his hand he threw himself flat, as indeed his colleague had already done. Not that this availed much, for as the rock struck its opposite number al the base of the buried Ultra there came an overwhelming explosion, exactly like the one that Abna had unwittingly created in the underworld. Then, slowly, came quietness with radioactive dust and smoke floating away on the breeze.

With a grim chuckle, Agos Thar tugged off his goggles and surveyed the scene.

"I am sorry, my friends, that your space machine has been so ingloriously eliminated," he commented cynically, tossing the goggles on one side. "Until you are needed again you will join the workers of the underworld and labor in our magnificent quest."

The four rose promptly and walked to the great yawning hole, which was the entrance to the underworld. They passed through it into the intense gloom, walking sure-footedly one behind the other, never once speaking, obeying implicitly the order they had been given.

They looked neither right nor left, their main desire being to mine rock and bring it to the surface, and destroy anybody who tried to prevent them.

How they entered the busy underworld or were absorbed into the vast army of zombie-workers they had no idea. The awareness of events was sharp enough at the time, but afterwards the impression faded and they were left with the realization of having to work and endure the tails of a lash if they slacked for an instant. For there were uniformed guards down here who everlastingly prowled and wreaked death or injury on those whom they thought were not working at full pressure.

Days, weeks, maybe even months, and the Crusaders never spoke to each other, so utterly in subjection were their personalities. This state of affairs would have continued indefinitely had not the unexpected happened.

The Crusaders were all in one particular section of workers, toiling like them in the removal of rocks from their natural bed. Like all the other gangs, they were watched constantly by one or other of the guards. On one of these occasions the guard seemed particularly interested in Viona. The sight of her industrious young figure, the grace and suppleness she epitomized, combined with her coppery hair and attractive features seemed to stir his baser passions. That she was a woman of another world did not matter: She was young and, despite the enforced dullness of her mind, alluring, and that was enough for him.

Viona realized this when, in the middle of her work, she suddenly found the guard at her side, his powerful arm gripping her around the waist. He grinned at her as she stared in wonder.

"You know the English language, the language of your planet, and so do I," he explained. "There are ways in which you can get out of this hell-hole... All you've got to do is be nice to me."

Viona did not answer. She felt herself drawn closer as the massive forearm tightened. She wanted to use her own strength to tear free of him, but once again the iron compulsion made her helpless.

"Surely it should not be difficult to be nice to me, to earn your freedom?" the guard murmured, his face close to hers.

He stopped, suddenly aware of two violet eyes staring at him in cold frenzy from nearby. The Amazon had stopped pulling at a rock to watch him, and now something was stirring inside her as she saw Viona pinned helplessly against him. What the emotion was the Amazon did not know, but it was probably the instinct of mother-love, the desire to protect her own, piercing through the dense fog of mental compulsion that surrounded her.

Abna and Mexone stared, too, but they did not act. The breakthrough had not come to them as it had to the Amazon.

"Let that girl alone," the Amazon whispered at last, her every word a threat. "She's my daughter, not a plaything for your dirty hands."

The guard grinned and put his other arm about Viona's waist. The pressure he exerted was so tremendous she gave a sobbing gasp of pain, and that was enough for the Amazon. The tigress in her crashed through the compulsion barrier and she hurtled forward in one of her catlike springs.

The guard turned in slow annoyance as he heard the Amazon behind him, but he did not loose his crushing hold of Viona; at least not then. A second later he had to as the Amazon's fist crashed into his face, sending him reeling backwards. As it happened, he did not entirely lose his balance for he collided with one of the big drilling machines. He gripped it, shook his spinning head fiercely, and then used the machine to spring himself back into action.

Just in time the Amazon whirled away from Viona and stood ready for the onslaught. The guard arrived with the violence of a 10-ton truck, and with like violence he came to a stop, his head jarred backwards by the iron impact of the Amazon's knuckles. Nor did she stop there: she rained blow after blow on him as he tried to dodge her onslaught.

Finally, half the senses thrashed out of him, he crashed over on the dusty, rocky floor, his hands flung out helplessly in front of him, and that action jerked him back to alertness. Quite unexpectedly his hand closed over a heavy metal bar used for prizing rock out of the walls. In that moment he had a weapon, and he turned it to account as the Amazon plunged on him. Just in time she saw the bar and sidestepped impalement on it by the very force of her onrush. With a jerk she slowed up and then spun around at incredible speed even while the guard was struggling painfully to his feet. Instantly she had grasped the bar and held its full length in both her hands, her fingers gripping each end.

"Quite clever, my friend," she said coldly, her violet eyes smoldering. "But you weren't quick enough, were you?"

The others looked on dumbly.

The guard remained silently uneasy, watching the Amazon. He moved a little as with a sudden effort the Amazon started bending the metal bar as simply as an ordinary person might bend a warm candle.

"There!" she said finally, critically surveying the metal 'U' imprisoned between her hands. "Quite an excellent collar for you, my friend."

Before the guard could grasp what was coming, the Amazon jumped to his side and flung the 'U' over his head and shoulders. It dropped to his neck, and once there, the Amazon began to tighten the ends of the bar, pushing the two ends over each other and thereby forming a tightening noose of metal.

The guard tore frantically and uselessly at the 'collar' which was choking the life out of him, but his strength was not equal to straightening the bar one fraction of an inch. Once he realized this he flung himself on the Amazon in sheer blind fury and panic. Quickly she dodged, but not quite soon enough. The bar struck her across the back of the head with numbing force, straight upon a nerve center. She blacked out immediately and crashed to her face, her head half buried in a pile of loose chippings.

Viona, Mexone and Abna, still not free of compulsion, could do nothing but gaze dully, and so indeed did the workers. They all watched the guard slowly strangle and die in his garroting collar; then they turned and looked at the sprawled Amazon with her head half buried in the stone chippings. Each member of the Crusaders knew that something ought to be done, but they could not determine what... So they continued to wait, only resuming work as other guards glanced in their direction. But the other guards did not come and investigate. So far as they knew, and could see, everything was normal. The distance was too great for them to detect the strangled guard on the ground.

Then, at last, the Amazon began to move. The momentarily numbed nerve center reasserted itself and life began to return. She pulled herself out of the stone chippings and considered the situation—considered something particularly which had happened to herself. She felt incredibly normal, sharply intelligent, devoid of senseless rage, fully able to plan her next move. In a word, she was as she had always been, without a trace of overpowering compulsion.

Since the power of reason had returned, she used it to the full, even as she surveyed the strangled guard and the quietly working Viona, Abna and Mexone. Yet, even as she weighed things, she felt her mind slipping again as waves of compulsion began to eat their way into her brain. She frowned. The momentary deadening of the nerve centers of her brain could not have brought the strange surcease from domination, so there must be another reason... And there seemed to her to be only one answer.

Abruptly, before her mind became too cloudy, she flung herself back into the stone chippings, dragging them once more over her head and allowing just enough room to breathe. Here she remained, motionless, for quite a while.

She realized that something had happened, an incredible and wonderful thing! The compulsion had ceased. She could not feel it any more. Nor had she felt it since the moment she had buried herself in the chippings. She smiled to herself and then slowly began to emerge again. Immediately the compulsion came back, but only weakly. She was complete master of it, and herself, at least for the present.

She acted immediately, taking advantage of the fact that there was no surveillance to worry over at the moment. As fast as possible she seized Viona and thrust her on the floor, burying her head in the chippings… Then, as the dazed girl at length emerged, Abna was treated to the same procedure. And finally Mexone. The task finished, the four stood looking at each other in perplexity.

"What's happened?" Viona asked at last. "I feel almost normal again. Just a bit of mental perturbation, but I can easily offset it. At least for a while."

"For about eight hours, as near as I can calculate," the Amazon answered quickly. "That's about as long as our wills can remain superior to the compulsion, then back we'll go under the influence. I don't know how it is, but these chippings act as an insulator to the extremely short waves of thought. I found it by accident, and I don't have to tell you that we're going to take enormous advantage of it."

"No question about that," Abna confirmed grimly.

"We'll make rough helmets," the Amazon went on, glancing about her. "We'll use our own judgment as to when to use them, but we ought to be able to keep our minds more or less free from compulsion for quite a long time to come. Naturally we'll play dumb as far as our captors are concerned."

Mexone looked troubled. "Quite a good idea, Amazon, but where does it get us in the end? We can't beat the mob in control of this underworld, and we've lost the Ultra, so we can't escape into space. Just what are we going to do?"

"I'll think it out as I go along," the Amazon replied briefly. "Even if we've nowhere to escape to we can at least die gloriously. These zombies want freeing, and that sadist of an Agos Tbar wants teaching a lesson. Those are our main objectives. We'll think of something, even if we have to steal a spaceship to make good our escape into the void—That's all." The Amazon broke off abruptly. "Somebody's coming. Act dumb just as before."

Instantly the four changed their expressions to dumb vagueness and drifted back mechanically to their former tasks of hauling forth rock and stacking it in neat piles, as did the rest of the zombies. As they did so, a couple of guards from one of the other sections came to investigate. Plainly they were puzzled and furious at discovering one of their number dead. Between them they managed to pull away the garroting metal bar, then one of them turned to the Amazon, bringing her to attention by a slash of his whip.

"What do you know about this?" he demanded pointing to the dead guard. But all he received was a dull stare of the violet eyes, while Abna, Viona and Mexone went on working tensely.

"Answer me!" the guard commanded, felling the Amazon to the floor with one blow of his powerful arm. "Who did this?"

The Amazon did not answer; and in fact nobody did. The guard used his whip with devilish force, but the Amazon took the lash across her back and made no effort to retaliate—which was fortunate for the guard, otherwise he would have suffered a broken neck for his pains.

"Why waste time?" the other guard asked finally. "We'll get nothing out of them, and possibly they didn't do it. I don't see how they could, the way their minds are held." In the end the matter was dropped. The dead guard was picked up and carried away, and after a while a new guard took his place. Probably the matter was reported, but certainly nothing more was heard of it.

The Crusaders took action of sorts when their shift ended. Each managed to conceal and take away some of the precious chippings, and this performance they repeated every time their shift ended. Though they were imprisoned with other zombies during their 'off time' and sleeping period, this was really no detriment since the poor devils were too dull to apprehend what was going on and usually slept heavily all through their rest period.

Not so the Crusaders. Little by little each of them fashioned a small cap, using rough fabric from the thousands of waste-rags lying around the underworld, and gluing the stone chippings in pebble-dash fashion to the cloth. It was a slow and sticky business, the adhesive being a gummy, tenacious product used as a by-product in the general slave business of mining rocks, ores, and, in places, crude oil.

In a fortnight each Crusader had a protective cap, easily carried in their tights, and on every possible occasion they were worn.

Gradually the constant nullification of the compulsion waves gave the Crusaders comparative independence, enough for them to run eight to nine hours at a stretch under their own will power. The more they used the caps the more their wills exerted themselves.

Then at last came a change. The arrogant Agos Thar returned on the scene, accompanied by a couple of guards. It was only about an hour after the quartet had commenced their daily shift when he arrived, so they were quite clear mentally and full of expectation for a change in their modus operandi before very long.

For quite a time Thar stood watching their activities, then with a crack of his vicious whip he brought their endeavors to an abrupt stop. He stood measuring them with his merciless eyes, and they for their part gazed dully toward him, fighting down the overpowering desire to explode into vengeful rage. Particularly the Amazon, with whom the memory of the dead Thania was still a dominant thing.

"So, my friends, I gather that by now you have learned sense," Thar commented dryly. "The time has arrived for you to carry out the project for which you have been selected."

"You mean," the Amazon asked haltingly, "the—the kindling of your dead sun?"

"That is exactly what I mean. You know the route into space— you know precisely what has to be done. As I said before, to you four belongs the honor of bringing the sun back to our system, and afterwards I and my colleagues will expand in power to limits as yet undreamed of."

Silence. Fixed, uncomprehending stares. Thar stared, too, for a moment, as though he were trying to read something from the deadpan faces. When he did not succeed, he motioned briefly.

"The time is now," he said curtly. "A space machine has been brought for you, one that will never be needed again since, as you already know, this is to be a one-way journey."

A signal followed and the two attending guards sprang into action with their guns ready. The Amazon gave Abna and the others a brief, knowing glance and then started to walk, mechanically, through the busy zombie-like industry of the underworld until finally the surface was gained.

The first thing the four saw as they continued marching was the outline of two fairly large spaceships, and toward the nearest of these they were directed by the guards, Agos Thar coming up in the rear. When the spaceship was reached he called a halt and smiled—that hard, relentless smile.

"I am aware," he said, "that this must seem an inglorious end for you, presumably so mighty in your achievements. But console yourselves with the honor of what you are doing. Now listen carefully and let the final instructions sink into your brains.

"That ship you are about to enter is loaded with equal proportions of negative and positive rock. I call it that for convenience. You will travel to the dead sun and never alter speed. All you will do is set the course on minus nine and drive without halt. Our mathematics show that you will finally strike the dead sun directly across a range of rock, which rock is in turn linked up with all the other rock on the dead sun's face. The outcome of that should be plain to you: Instant fusion and an atomic holocaust in which you will perish."

Silence. Four pairs of eyes stared dully and fixedly.

"You understand the orders?" Thar snapped.

"We understand the orders," the Amazon assented deliberately. "We travel on course minus nine without alteration of speed."

"Correct... Now depart."

The Amazon turned from the airlock and entered the control room. With like deliberation Abna, Viona and Mexone followed her. Only when the airlock was closed did Abna expel a long sigh of relief.

"Keeping control over one's emotions in the face of provocation is the hardest job ever," he commented. "If he'd have said much more I'm afraid I'd have gummed the works up by knocking him down."

"Fortunate that you didn't," the Amazon murmured; then after a quick survey of the instrument board and its layout she grasped what was obviously the power switch and pulled it over.

Instantly there was a blasting roar from the power plant and the spaceship hurtled skywards with tremendous velocity, sending the four staggering backwards with the acceleration. Then suddenly a click and, automatically, gravity-nullifiers came into operation, producing more tolerable conditions.

Recovering her balance, the Amazon checked the control panel, set the pointer on the course-guide to minus-nine, and then turned to face the others.

They watched her as she pulled her small insulating rock cap from a pocket in her tights and placed it on her head.

"You'd better do the same," she advised. "We can't afford to take chances, and the nearer we are to that so-called civilized planet the more severe will be the compulsion effect."

The others put their caps on and then Abna glanced at the Amazon curiously.

"So far, Vi," he said, "you've done exactly as Thar ordered. But surely we're not going to continue to that dead star on the directed course?"

"Most certainly we're not," Mexone said decisively. "We've got a spaceship of sorts and mental freedom, so there's nothing to prevent us getting away into space and escaping this system forever, granting the fuel will give us the chance."

The Amazon shrugged. "As to that, I don't know—but I do know that there are two things to be done before we depart. First, we have to avenge Thania and ourselves in the fullest measure; and secondly, we have to bring some measure of freedom to those poor devils of zombies. To that end we are dedicated. Right?"

The others nodded slowly.

"Right!" the Amazon said. "We're not going to that sun as directed: We're going to deliver an ultimatum to the government of the 'civilized' planet from which Agos Thar comes. We're going to make certain demands, and we're going to see that they are satisfied."

"How can we be sure of that?" Abna questioned. "We might be attacked even as we approach the planet."

The Amazon smiled coldly. "I think not, Abna. They won't be anxious to attack this vessel which Thar assured us is loaded with positive and negative rock. What I propose to do is issue the ultimatum, and if it is not obeyed we will drop our entire content of positive and negative rock on the planet. Inevitably the planet will be almost, if not completely, destroyed. I don't doubt that our orders will be complied with to the letter."

"And what are they?" Viona asked curiously.

"Agos Thar is to come with us to the dead sun and be present at the rekindling. He has carefully avoided that suicidal performance, but he's not going to escape so easily. In fact," the Amazon added, clenching her yellow fist, "he's not going to escape at all. Once we get him to the dead star we'll leave him to do the rekindling as best he can. If he does not do it, he will perish for lack of food, means of escape, and so forth. We ourselves will escape and return to the civilized planet and find some means of making the government thereof adopt a more tolerant attitude to the zombies."

There was a long silence; then Viona spoke.

"It's obvious you have made your mind up, mother, so I for one am not going to question your judgment. Go ahead... There's just one thing, though."

"And what's that?"

"Suppose, instead of returning to the civilized world and letting them see we've escaped, we go instead to the ghost world and instruct the zombies in the art of using the pebble helmets? We only need to show a few of them, restore them to normal, and they'll be able to do the rest themselves. Once cut off from the mental compulsion, they'll be able to rise again in full power, even more so with a sadist like Agos Thar wiped out."

The Amazon nodded. "Good idea, Viona. Much better than mine. Right, first let's check up how much rock we have on board."

This was a comparatively simple matter and revealed the surprising fact that nearly three-quarters of the vessel, in the storage holds, was loaded with the deadly cargo.

Somewhat sobered by her appraisal, the Amazon led the way back into the control room and glanced through the window. The disc of the dead star, their intended destination if Thar had his way, was as yet a long way off and only faintly discernable. But the mass of the civilized planet was not too distant. An hour's flight would bring it close.

"Well, here we go!" the Amazon said decisively, turning from a contemplation of the leering face in the void. "From here on I fancy Agos Thar is in for an uncomfortable time. He will not be allowed to forget Thania—ever!"

CHAPTER 4

A star reborn

The Amazon changed the course of the spaceship and swung its nose toward the 'civilized' planet; then she began a search for and presently found a television transmitter-receiver.

At first, when they turned it on, they got only flashing pictures and a continuous high-pitched shriek in the sound system. Then finally the picture they were fishing for became steady, and the shriek disappeared into a deep bass hum of power.

There was a man on the screen, attired in light and easy clothing. After a fashion he was not at all bad looking. At the moment he was staring in bewilderment into his own screen, evidently seeing a picture of the Amazon's and Abna's faces, with a view of spaceship control room behind them.

Suddenly he spoke, in the urgent gibberish. The Amazon cut him short and moved forward so that only she was visible on the screen.

"Find somebody who understands my language," she said, slowly and deliberately, and hoped that she would be understood. To her surprise the man gave a quick reply.

"I understand your language perfectly, as do others in authority here. Are you not the Golden Amazon?"

"I am," the Amazon assented. "I have an urgent message for your governing body, or ruler, or whatever he is. Let me converse with him."

The operator nodded, got up from his chair and went out of the picture. The Amazon glanced at the others.

"Take control of this vessel, Abna, while I talk," she ordered. "Bring it to an orbit above the 'civilized' planet, then drop down into its atmosphere and then keep on going very slowly in a circuit of the globe, at about 1,000 feet so we can be seen."

Abna nodded and turned to the controls. Viona and Mexone stood together, watching the television screen. Presently there appeared on it a white-haired, patriarchal-looking man with sad dark eyes. He studied the screen bearing the image of the Amazon's face, and then spoke in a soft, pleasing voice.

"I am President Semna, the recognized ruler of the major country of this planet. I understand you are the Golden Amazon of far-distant Earth."

"You understand correctly." The Amazon was polite, but frigid. She was trying to decide in her own mind whether she liked this man with the tired dark eyes or not. It surprised her to discover that she had no feelings of resentment toward him. His personality projected itself as kindly and tolerant, which was a decided surprise.

"I have a proposition to put to you, President Semna," the Amazon continued. "In fact, it's more than a proposition: It's an ultimatum. I dislike forcing it upon you, but I'm afraid the blame that makes it necessary lies with Commander Agos Thar, who, I understand, is your scientific adviser as well as being an important number in your military force."

President Semna gave a tired smile. "You have designated Agos Thar correctly, Amazon. He is also a despot—or have you gathered that already?"

"That is exactly what I've gathered," the Amazon assented, "though I must confess to surprise at hearing you admit the fact. One would have thought that—"

"Agos Thar has the whole of this planet under his domination," Semna interrupted anger coming into his fine eyes. "He has gained that position by lies, trickery, and a complete disregard for he feelings of others. I am the president, yes, but I am nothing more than a figurehead, and my life is in constant danger. Thar alone rules and behind him are all the unwanted elements of our society He has had control for many years. I had hopes when you and your friends arrived from outer space that there would be a change, but I realize I was wrong. From what I have heard, you and those with you have fallen before him."

"You underestimate us," the Amazon said, with a grim smile.

"At the moment we're supposed to be making a suicide leap to your dead sun, for the purpose of rekindling it. A worthy cause, no doubt, but it doesn't warrant committing suicide to bring it about when long-distance remote control instruments could do it just as easily. Nor does it warrant the slavery of a neighbor planet and the destruction of their way of life. In those things Agos Thar has succeeded so far, but he has a score to settle, not only for his brutality in general but for his cold disregard of the death of one of our number."

Semna sighed and gave a shrug. "I am afraid, Amazon, that murder—and things even worse than murder—rest but lightly on Agos Thar's shoulders. As to the rest, I am not acquainted with all the details. Perhaps you would enlighten me?"

The Amazon did so, giving all the facts. The only thing she suppressed was the discovery of the nullifying stone chippings. Semna listened with dignified silence to all she had to say, then he spread his hands.

"And what, Amazon, do you imagine you can do? What right have you to speak of an ultimatum? By your own admission, Thar has caused one of your number to die, and he has blasted your space machine into dust. He has even sent you on the suicide trip to rekindle our sun. Just what can you do about it? I gather you have found a way to circumvent the compulsion waves which Thar himself controls, but even that does not give you freedom."

"You overlook the fact that we could escape into space and leave this system far behind," the Amazon said.

Semna shook his maned head. "I think not, Amazon, even though I wish for your sake that that were possible. This planet has telescopic eyes watching the void around it all the time. You could never escape. Thar would not be so lax as to let you."

After a moment the Amazon asked: "Where is Agos Thar at the moment?"

"In his own headquarters. He has not been back long from his journey to what you call the zombie world."

"Then here is my ultimatum. He will join us here, he alone, in this ship and come with us to rekindle the sun. If we are to die in the attempt, then so must he. With his passing maybe you will be able to become a president in more than name only."

Semna gave his tired smile. "You know he will never comply

with an order like that, Amazon. He'll turn his forces—"

The Amazon cut in: "If he doesn't obey, there's a load of positive and negative rock waiting to fall on your planet. Quite enough to blast it to powder. That he knows full well. He must come with us or your planet ceases to be. Since he chooses to be ruthless, so shall we be. I am sorry for you, president, and those on your world who are innocent, but there it is. You can see now why Thar won't attack us. That would be a sure way of blasting both him and his world."

President Semna's face had sobered considerably. He began to nod slowly. "Yes, Amazon, I understand completely. Obviously, there is nothing I can do except have Commander Thar brought here to receive your ultimatum."

"As soon as you can," the Amazon snapped. "And if you doubt anything I've said, have your telescopes trained on the void around your planet. They'll be bound to pick us up, since we're not very far away."

The president got up and disappeared from the screen. The Amazon gave a glance at Abna. "How far away are we from the planet, Abna?"

"No more than 1,500 miles. We'll be there in no time. After that I'll keep circling until you tell me differently."

The Amazon nodded and glanced at the blank screen, then through the outlook window at the 'civilized' planet looming close. It gave her a momentary thrill of satisfaction to realize that she had the mastery of the situation—that in her hands was the power to destroy the planet instantly if she so chose.

Then before she could think much further along these lines, Agos Thar appeared on the screen, uniformed as usual, his hard eyes peering from under the shiny peak of his uniform cap. For a moment or two his expression was vaguely puzzled as he looked at the small insulating cap on the Amazon's blonde head. Then he spoke:

"So, Amazon, you have issued an ultimatum? I am to join you, or be destroyed with my planet it I refuse?"

"I can hardly put it plainer," the Amazon retorted. "You will board this vessel as rapidly as possible, making an airlock to airlock transference."

Thar hesitated for a moment, then said: "I am intelligent enough to grasp when the situation is against me, Amazon, but it is only a temporary set-back, I assure you. You intend to commit suicide in the rekindling of our sun, I believe, and you also intend that I shall die with you. Surely you don't think I am fool enough to believe that you will sacrifice your lives when, obviously, you have a chance to escape? Sacrifice mine, yes, but not your own."

The Amazon did not answer the question. Instead she made a statement. "We will give you one hour to get here. Thar. If you are not here by then, the entire contents of this ship will be dropped on your planet. That is all."

Decisively, she switched off and then relaxed in her chair. Viona came over slowly to her.

"Think he'll come?" she asked, and the Amazon gave a grim smile.

"He'll come; but if he doesn't, he knows what the consequences will be."

"You really mean it, don't you? Quite determined to blow the planet up if he doesn't comply."

The Amazon shrugged. "Quite determined. The planet is a pesthole, and therefore ripe for destruction. President Semna may be liberal minded now, but don't forget his planet has enslaved the zombies for centuries. That's the only way to look at it. The innocent will suffer for the guilty, I know, but that can't he helped."

"Do you think we'll escape the explosion?" Mexone asked.

"I've no doubt of it. We'll drop the load from 200 miles: The force of gravity will drag the rock down to the planet."

"Might they not burn up in the atmosphere?"

"No. You're overlooking the fact that—unlike meteors from outer space—they won't have any initial velocity worth speaking of when they leave our ship. After that they'll move downwards so fast the atmosphere of the planet won't have time to convert the rocks into meteorites…" The Amazon paused and then gave a grim smile. "But why work out the details? Thar will come all right."

And the Amazon was right. Thirty minutes later, by which time the spaceship had slowed to a crawl in its constant circuit of the planet, there came into view a second spaceship, apparently a small, one-man affair. Very shortly it had come alongside and immediately magnetic grapples came into operation, producing a vacuum tightness from airlock to airlock. Only then did the Amazon throw the switch that opened the door, and as the thick metal cover slowly swung aside she stood ready for whatever untoward action might arise. But there was none. Evidently Thar was not taking any risks.

He came from one ship to the other along the narrow tunnel, and then stood grimly waiting. Abna, Viona and Mexone kept a wary eye on him while the Amazon closed the airlock and then switched off the magnetic grapples.

"Well, I'm here," Thar snapped, tossing down his uniform cap on the table. "What happens now?"

"We travel to the dead sun," the Amazon said coldly. "When we are there we will act further. Until then it would be best if you behaved yourself."

Thar smiled sardonically. "I can hardly do anything else." He wandered to a fixed chair nearby and sat down. He was still smiling to himself as though enjoying a hidden joke. Then he said: "I have to admit that you are far cleverer than I'd ever realized. I assume that your immunity from radiation has something to do with those crude caps you're wearing?"

"Precisely," the Amazon responded brusquely; then she turned to the switchboard and busied herself with it, swinging the small vessel gradually around until it was heading away from Thar's planet into the remoter deeps. Dimly, ahead, cutting out the stars with its gray circle, loomed the dead sun toward which they were heading.

Presently Agos Thar asked a question: "Are there any particular rules of behavior during this trip, Amazon? What, for instance, am I expected to do?"

The Amazon turned and looked at him stonily. "I am not in the least concerned what you do, Thar. I will tell you this much: During your journey to this sun of yours you will be treated as one of ourselves—given food and allowed to sleep. But none of us will speak to you. If you make any attempt to interfere with our activities you'll be instantly stopped. We ourselves will rest in turns so that two of us are always watching you. Understand?"

"Perfectly." Thar looked ironically amused. "I wonder how you intend to deal with me if I choose to get fractious? You have no weapons, and there are certainly none aboard this vessel."

The Amazon said: "We have our hands, and as you know already, we can use those very effectively."

Thar shrugged and made no comment. He relaxed into a mood of deep introspection, and remained in it throughout the journey.

There came the moment when the spaceship touched down and became still on the dark, slaggy surface of the mighty globe that had once been a sun. The engine ceased its humming.

The Amazon said: "We have this rock to transport outside, Abna, and it's too dangerous a job to allow Thar to help us: He might throw away his life and ours. Better chain him to the switchboard while we get busy."

Abna nodded, seized the coldly smiling Thar with massive hands, and impelled him out of the chair to the main panel. Chain and handcuffs took care of the rest.

This done, the Amazon went over to a big locker on the farther wall and pulled open the doors. She nodded in satisfaction and tugged out four spacesuits. After she had handed them over, she considered for a moment or two, then pulled out yet another one and threw it contemptuously at Thar's feet. He looked at it coldly, then back to her.

"You'll need it later," she explained briefly. "You're not going to have the easy death of airless cold, my friend: You've got the life of Thania to pay for."

The others said nothing. They had often seen the Amazon in a cold mood, but never so cold as this. Quietly, like the Amazon herself, they scrambled into their spacesuits, tested the radio communicators on their backs, and then finally the Amazon opened the emergency lock in the side of the ship.

It was double-chambered, like the one on the lost Ultra, so arranged that the inner lock had to be closed before the outer lock could be opened, thus preventing any escape of air into the absolute vacuum of space outside.

There was no longer need or opportunity for saying anything, and Agos Thar merely watched attentively as the Crusaders went about their task of unloading the ship of its dangerous rock load.

It was a job that took nearly two hours to accomplish. Then, when the last of the rocks had been brought out, the Amazon surveyed the landscape through her transparent helmet. Her voice could be heard in the earphones of the others as they stood around her.

"We've done all we need to do here, and have rid ourselves of our terribly dangerous cargo. The rest is up to Agos Thar. He will be brought out here, and left. He can either die gloriously re-kindling this sun, or he can die of starvation. It's up to him. Either way it doesn't matter."

"And suppose somebody comes and rescues him?" Viona questioned.

"Do you think he's loved enough for anybody to do that?" the Amazon countered.

"No—but it could happen by accident. The ruler of the civilized planet is expecting this sun to rekindle, and ourselves to be involved in the holocaust along with Thar. When it doesn't happen he might have an investigation made, Thar might be found, and we're back where we started."

The Amazon thought for a moment before she spoke.

"We'll leave this for fate to decide. We'll take one piece of rock away with us, which is quite harmless by itself. Then we'll travel to a distance of 500 miles and release it. Given an initial impetus, the gravitation of this huge dead star will do the rest. The rock will not lose anything from friction for there is no air to encounter. If it strikes its opposite number a sun will flash into being. If, however, it strikes material akin to itself, nothing will happen and Thar might escape after all." The Amazon clenched her huge, gloved hand. "But I don't think that will happen. A man like Agos Thar won't go on living. Providence would not permit it."

After a moment Abna said: "You've relieved my mind a lot. Vi. The whole thing doesn't savor so much of plain cold murder if we leave it to chance to decide. After all, no matter what Thar may have done, we are not true Crusaders if we kill him outright." Then before the Amazon could reply, Abna went on: "Let's bring him out here and get it over with."

He started moving back to the ship, the others following him at a less urgent pace. Thar was unshackled from the switchboard, given a spacesuit to don and then was shoved outside under the cold stars. He was made to walk about 200 yards, then the Amazon called a halt.

Thar turned and waited passively, the thumbs of his hands latched to his enormous, instrument-laden belt.

"You are entitled to know what is going to happen to you," the Amazon said. "Your fate is to be left to chance. You may survive, and you may not. Here is what we intend to do..." And with great deliberation she outlined the scheme that had been decided upon.

Thar listened without interruption, his face smiling coldly behind the transparent visor. He fiddled a good deal with the instruments on his belt but the quartet facing him merely thought this was a nervous reaction—until something utterly unexpected happened. It came just as the Amazon was at the end of explaining the position. Her words were truncated by a sudden violent vibration, transmitted through the ground.

Instantly she swung around in amazement, as also did Abna, Viona and Mexone. None of them had heard actual sound, since they were in a complete vacuum: All they sensed was a mighty vibration, which had its center in a huge cascade of sparks climbing upward toward the stars. Becoming remoter—and remoter.

Slowly the stunned quartet realized what had happened. The small spaceship in which they had made the journey to here had somehow taken off on its own.

Then came laughter in the helmet phones—the utter mirth of somebody enjoying a tremendous joke. Obviously Agos Thar. The four turned back slowly to look at him. He was standing now with legs straddled, a piece of rock in his gloved hands.

"Naturally, you did not expect that?" he demanded, between gales of laughter. "The great ones, the supreme scientific geniuses, were caught out completely! And yet so simple a trick. The engines of the spaceship are controlled both manually and by radio remote control. Here on my belt is a radio activator, just as there is one on each of your belts. I managed to set and press my radio button and the ship took off. It isn't following any decided course because I had no time to fix that, but at least it's gone into space out of your reach. Clever, eh?"

The Amazon glanced at the starry abyss into which the space machine had gone. She looked at the distant leering face. Then she caught the bitter glances of the others.

"All right," she said quietly, shrugging. "So you won the last trick after all, Thar. What happens now?"

"Death! Death for all of us in the mighty holocaust of this sun when it is touched off. I will die and you, too—all of you, a just revenge for your effort to try to kill me. Nobody will ever attempt to rescue me: I am too hated on my planet for that to happen. And, for your part, there is nobody to save you. The only one who might have done so is dead, and your ship is destroyed. We have it to ourselves, my friends, and with this rock in my hand, I am the judge and arbiter of your fate."

The four did not say anything. Fixedly they watched for what Agos Thar would do next...and his actions somewhat surprised them.

For suddenly he turned, the rock still in his hand, and hurried to the nearest towering hill of rock and began to climb it slowly. After a while his voice came as he paused for a moment.

"You wonder what I'm doing? I'll tell you, my clever friends. I am going to climb to the top of this hill and then toss down this piece of rock. The moment it strikes this hillside of 'opposite number' rock the holocaust and death will come. I intend to do it when I am ready, when I have driven your nerves to breaking point... And there is no way out for you!" The voice rose to a hysterical shout in the helmet phones. "If you try to shoot me down I shall simply fall and the rock will go just the same. You think you haven't the weapons to shoot me, but you have. Those barreled instruments on your belts are guns, not drills, as you probably think. Another trick lost, clever ones, another trick!"

With that final outburst, Thar resumed climbing.

The quartet on the plain, bitterly conscious of their helplessness, watched him go, catching their breath at intervals as he slipped or slid in his haste. But never once did he let go of the rock—and so finally he reached the top of the hill; an almost remote puppet figure 300 feet above.

"Now, my friends, prepare yourselves!" His voice came quite clearly over the radio. "I regret only one thing; that you will not have the time to think of the death that is about to befall you. It will be over all too quickly. The moment this rock falls to this hill on which I stand, ignition will take place and that will be the end! Watch! Watch closely!"

Even as he gave the order, Thar began to raise the chunk of rock on high. The four moved to the base of the hill and stared up at him.

"I'm afraid there's no answer to this," Abna said grimly. "For the first time in our lives we're caught out. There isn't even time to work it out in metaphysics—"

"What's the matter with him?" Viona asked suddenly, pointing. "He's looking at something. See!"

The others saw in a moment what Viona meant. Suddenly, for a reason best known to himself, Thar had ceased raising the rock. His arm had dropped again and the rock was in his hand. His whole attitude was tense as he stared at something beyond the vision of the quartet—something that was evidently in the sky, to judge from the attitude of the lone figure on the hilltop.

Over the top of the hill, almost over Agos Thar himself, a monstrous gray shape moving at fair speed became abruptly visible. It seemed unendingly long as it cleaved through the starry heaven, its many outlook windows ablaze with light.

"The Ultra!" screamed the voice of Mexone, in utter disbelief.

The others did not answer, because they could not. With their own eyes they had seen the Ultra blown up—and besides, there was something else gripping their attention. A long grappling chain trailing from the Ultra's base.

They realized what the idea was even as Thar himself must have done so. His lone figure twirled suddenly on the summit of the hill as he made a dive for the lower reaches. But he was seconds too late. The swinging grappling chain struck him on the back of the head as he made to descend from the ridge, and instantly he was flung like a bullet into space, his scream in the helmet phones nearly splitting the eardrums of the four who heard—and watched.

"The rock!" Viona yelled suddenly, and dived forward like one gone mad.

For once her brain reacted more quickly than that of her mother, father or Mexone. For as Thar was swept to death from the hillside, the rock was naturally released from his grip and ejected forward as he hurtled, his helmet and skull crushed like eggshell, into space.

Never in her life had Viona moved so fast. Her eyes were on that white chunk as it came sailing downwards. Chippings of stone flew under her great boots, her arms thrust outwards as she stumbled and ran with breakneck speed. She felt as though her heart were bursting as the rock thudded down into her outstretched forearms, numbing them with the impact. She tripped, gulped, and fell over, with the rock clutched to her. There she lay, gulping breath from the spacesuit's air containers and shaking with the ague of fright and enormous exertion.

The others came up quickly and Abna hauled her to her feet. She stood trembling, the deadly rock clutched to her.

"Good work, Viona," the Amazon said breathlessly. "We'd have been extinct by now if you hadn't moved as fast as you did."

"Yes..." Viona gave a huge gulp. "Yes... I know. Only the thickness of my body between the two rocks. Whew! I feel as though I've been turned inside out!"

"How did the Ultra get here?" Mexone demanded. "That's the part I can't understand."

"We will—and soon," the Amazon replied, watching the enormous spaceship as it cruised around in a vast circle, still trailing its length of grappling chain.

"It would seem that Agos Thar got his desserts, anyway," Abna remarked, presently taking his eyes from the Ultra. "I'll go and see what's left of him. I watched where he fell."

Turning, he went away up the hillside, and while he was gone the Ultra came down rather jerkily to the plain and then became still. Abna returned to the waiting three and shrugged his shoulders.

"Not a very pleasant sight," he commented. "Thar is completely dead, with half his head smashed in and his helmet completely gone. It looks as though—"

He stopped, staring with the others at the Ultra. The airlock had opened and a fan of light was casting outwards across the dark plain. Against the light stood one figure in a spacesuit, frantically waving.

"Can—can it possibly be Thania?" Abna exclaimed at length.

"Only one way to find out," the Amazon answered briefly, and set the example by moving toward the spaceship with the others following her.

In very short time the distance was covered and entry made into the big, familiar control room. The airlock was closed and the pressure restored to normal, then as the solitary controller of the giant spaceship struggled out of the enveloping spacesuit there was no longer any room for doubt. The gray, mischievous eyes, the tousled mop of blonde hair, the slimly girlish figure in space-slacks and a silk blouse. Yes, it was Thania all right.

"This," Abna remarked, as he, too, cast aside his spacesuit "seems a suitable moment to quote a famous Earth remark. 'Dr. Livingstone, I presume?' "

"I don't know what you men by that, Abna, but thank heaven I came in time," Thania responded. "As far as I could judge, Agos Thar was threatening you, wasn't he?"

"That," the Amazon said grimly, "is the biggest understatement I've heard yet. He was on the verge of creating an inferno, and in spite of your work with that grappling chain, he might have succeeded, though posthumously, had not Viona literally jumped to the occasion and saved all of us."

Thania looked puzzled. "How do you mean?"

As briefly as she could, the Amazon explained. Then she asked: "How does it happen that you appear like this, so providentially? Thar told us you were dead. He even examined you and said you were. Most certainly you looked it."

The girl looked mystified. "That I don't understand. I only know that I came to myself in the pit they had dug for me, as they did for you. I was terribly weary and my brain was buzzing with crazy notions. I must have been unconscious, yet strangely enough I found that I wasn't chained and that my body was free to move. There didn't seem to be anybody in sight, and the spaceships had disappeared. Somehow I managed to climb out of the pit and found the pits in which you others had been completely empty. I felt alone—terribly alone—and enormously scared.

"I surmised, rightly or wrongly, that you had been taken away somewhere but that I had been left behind for a reason unknown. So I investigated and found the Ultra under its ash covering. I got inside it, closed the airlock door, then operated the controls as I have seen you do so often. The Ultra took off into space, and at a distance of several thousand miles away I stopped to think what I ought to do."

"And then?" the Amazon questioned, as the girl paused.

"Well, then it seemed to me that my job was to find out what had happened to the rest of you. I was the only one who could possibly effect a rescue, the only one with a spaceship. And our own spaceship, the Ultra, at that. But where had you gone? That was my problem. First I restored myself to health with the various medicines we have on board. I ate, slept, and thought. And I could think clearly since inside this Ultra there is no effect from the mental radiations. I reasoned out what I must do, and it seemed that the only thing possible was to watch the ghost planet for some signs of you. I had arrived at the conclusion that probably you had been taken into the underworld of the zombies."

"A correct solution," the Amazon smiled.

"So I realized. I didn't approach the ghost planet for fear of being seen, so I remained where I was in space and kept the planet's surface under constant observation with the high-power telescope. Watching through it I eventually saw you, Agos Thar and others emerge to the surface. I saw you, but not Thar, take off into space. At a good distance I followed you as you headed to this dead sun. I saw you swing off to the civilized planet. I saw you pick up somebody from a small spaceship, and it was when you landed on the surface of this dead star and your spaceship suddenly took off without you, I realized something grim was probably about to happen. I could see that somebody else was with you, and could only guess at his identity. I took a chance and guessed it to be Agos Thar. What he intended I didn't know, but I knew he couldn't be up to any good. So I decided to act. I started the Ultra on the move to this dead star. As I was approaching I saw a lone figure on the top of one of the hills, a chunk of rock in his hand.

"I didn't quite know what to do," Thania finished worriedly. "I took the only chance and dropped a grapple chain from the floor trap. I had the computer calculate a course over the solitary figure, which was done in a matter of seconds, and the Ultra was automatically set on course. Then the chain knocked Thar off the hill. You know the rest."

"Splendid work," the Amazon said admiringly, putting an arm about the girl's youthful shoulders. "You acted with skill and courage, Thania—in fact, like a true Crusader. I'm proud of you, as I'm sure we all are."

The others nodded urgent acquiescence, but Thania gave a little shiver.

"I'm afraid I would have thought twice about that chain if I'd realized Thar was carrying a piece of rock which could have transformed this dead star into a raging sun."

"Providence was with you," the Amazon smiled. Then she began to look vaguely puzzled, and added: "I wish I could understand why Thar made such a mistake regarding your death, He unchained you to make a thorough examination, decided you were dead, and pitched you back into the pit as a corpse. Yet all that had really happened was that you had passed out."

"There's one answer," Abna mused. "And the only possible one. Thar once said that the anatomy of his race and ours is totally different, even though we look the same externally. It's possible that he felt for Thania's heart and pulses where there are none—felt in the wrong place, to put it bluntly, and because he detected no reaction he assumed she was dead. Her breathing would be extremely shallow due to her unconsciousness. It's the only answer."

"Yes, you're probably right," the Amazon agreed.

"That still leaves us with a problem," Viona pointed out. "We saw Thar blow up the Ultra. At least he thought—and we thought—he did."

"Perhaps I can answer that," Thania said. "When I was leaving the ghost world in the Ultra there was one of those brief but tremendous dust storms on the plain where the Ultra had been: I saw it from above. I would suggest that the dust piled up in a great hill over the spot where the Ultra had been, making things look almost as before. I assume Thar didn't examine the spot too closely?"

"He left it entirely to his men," the Amazon said. "Yes, that was probably it, Thania. He left too much to chance and blew up a ship that wasn't there."

"From all of which," Viona said, spreading her hands, "we can safely say that Agos Thar outsmarted himself. Good! It was no more than he deserved. And we're left with a problem on our hands.

What do we do now?"

"Finish the job we started," the Amazon answered curtly.

She crossed to the Ullra's television equipment and switched it on. After a moment or two the familiar station of the 'civilized' planet appeared on the screen.

"The Golden Amazon speaking," the Amazon said, as the operator's familiar face appeared on the screen. "I would like to have communication with your president."

"I will advise him, Amazon."

There was the usual brief delay and then the president appeared. He sat down and looked at the screen, a curious mixture of hope and bewilderment reflected in his dark eyes.

"I'm surprised to hear from you, Amazon," he said quietly. "I was more than convinced that Agos Thar would have found a way to dispose of you."

The Amazon smiled tautly. "The only person disposed of is himself, President Semna."

"He—he's dead?" There was sudden relief on the patriarchal face.

"Completely. On the dead star he hoped to make into a new sun. Which brings me to the reason for contacting you."

"I am entirely ready to listen to anything you have to say. You have given me wonderful news, Amazon, telling me of the death of Commander Thar. Perhaps at last I will have a chance to exert my authority with him out of the way."

"That is my hope, and belief, Mr. President. But first hear what I have to say. I am going to make conditions because, with such a man as you, I believe those conditions can be made and adhered to. You will appreciate that we, as Crusaders, have a task to finish before we can consider our obligations discharged?"

"Of course. Speak on."

"At the moment we are based on the dead star. It's all ready for touching off into an atomic holocaust, which will turn it into the sun you so desperately need. I am prepared to undertake that task from a safe distance, under certain conditions."

"Name them."

"You will immediately withdraw the platino-barium sulphide Face from the heavens and destroy the machines which hold your neighbor slave race in domination. They are to be set free. You understand?"

"Only too clearly." Semna gave his tired smile. "And I will do it willingly, Amazon. As you already know, I never did agree with Thar's ruthless policy. Yes, I will give the order now to have the machines destroyed and the Face removed."

The Amazon was silent for a long moment, her intense eyes searching the aged face. Then she nodded slowly.

"Yes, I believe you," she said quietly. "When I see the slave people emerge, your dead sun will be reborn, and we will depart, never to return."

Semna said seriously: "You have accomplished a great thing, you and your comrades of a far-off world. We shall never forget you for it."

"The rest, then, is up to you. Farewell."

With that the Amazon cut off the television instrument and glanced at the others.

"Nothing to do now but wait," she said. "We'd better start moving on to a point near the ghost world—near enough to be able to drop a message on it, anyway."

"Message?" Abna frowned as he glanced at her. "What message are you referring to?"

The Amazon glanced up from the notepad on which she was inscribing a message with a stylo, and smiled faintly. Instead of answering she put it face down on a scanning plate, and operated the computer linked to the Translation Machine. Within seconds it ejected a thin metal foil, covered with strange writing resembling hieroglyphics. Finally she put it in a container, screwed the cap tightly, and then explained.

"When the zombies come from the underworld, released from their mental bondage, it will not take them long to recover their former obviously good intelligence. The point I am making is that when that happens they will be able to read the message—written in their own language—that I've put in this capsule. It tells them briefly about the chippings, which, in bulk, form an insulation against terror waves. It gives them a weapon to fight with if at any time in the future they should be subjected again."

"Nice idea," Abna approved, though for myself I completely

trust President Semna."

The Amazon shrugged. "So, in general, do I. But it's always as well to be on the safe side. Right, then, that's settled. Let's get going."

Abna moved to the switchboard and operated the controls. At once the Ultra took off from the desolate plain and hurtled into the gulf. In a matter of hours, moving at well under quarter speed, it was within 50 miles of the ghost world, the five travelers looking down on the wrecked and tumbled civilization. Once again they had to play the waiting game...

Hours passed before anything happened, and then it was something that seemed to presage the fact that President Semna was going lo keep his word. For the Face, that sinister visage which for so long had terrorized an entire race, faded from sight. The void was clear, gleaming coldly with stars.

"Good," the Amazon approved. "Now for the last part of this interstellar drama..."

This, however, was a good deal longer in coming—a period reckoned in several spells of sleeping and eating. Then at last Viona, whose turn it was to be on the watch, gave an excited cry.

"They're coming!" she exclaimed. "Out of the underworld— dozens of them."

The others were not long in joining her, and for a time they watched the varicolored tide of people as they crawled out of the underworld, men and women in their right minds and plainly trying to grasp why terror and compulsion had been removed from them. Through the powerful telescope, which the Amazon turned upon them, their expressions were plainly visible, expressions that reflected both an overwhelming relief and wonder.

"They're sane enough," the Amazon said, peering intently through the eyepiece. "Drop that capsule, Viona. I want to make sure they pick it up."

Viona did as instructed. After a moment there was the click of the floor ejector and the tiny capsule dropped into space outside and was almost immediately lost to sight because of its smallness.

It evidently landed all right some time later—a small parachute being deployed from it—because the watchers saw the still multiplying people surge towards a given spot—and the Amazon, having the closest view of all, watched as a man picked the capsule up. He gazed in bewilderment above, then turned to speak to the throng jostling around him.

The Amazon smiled to herself and pushed the telescope to one side on its gimbals.

"They'll sort it out in time," she said. "Now we'd better keep our part of the bargain. Viona, stand by the frontal long-distance ejector."

Viona obeyed, and stood with her hand on the release button.

The Amazon nodded her satisfaction and gave further orders.

"Mexone, put that chunk of rock in the ejector-chamber ready for release. Abna, get busy on the computer and let me know when we have reached exactly 200 miles from the dead sun. Thania, take visual observation and report progress."

Then the Amazon pulled over the power lever and set the Ultra hurtling into the gulf in a gigantic curve until at length the nose was pointed toward the dead star.

"This is a matter of flawless timing," she said tensely, her eyes on the instruments. "I intend to cross that dead star at half the speed of light. When we have reached almost that speed we ought to be 200 miles away, which is enough for the gravity of the dead sun to claim the rock. But we've got to get clear when the blast goes. Right! Here we go!"

She switched the decelerators to maximum to counter the terrific drag set up by the velocity. Faster and faster still the Ultra sliced through the gulf. The dead star increased in size by leaps and bounds, visible as a dead gray circle with whiter spots where the hills of rock were lying.

"Two hundred!" Abna snapped at last.

"Fire!" the Amazon ordered simultaneously.

Viona pressed the ejector button and announced curtly: "Rock gone!"

The Amazon snapped a switch and purple blinds shot up over the windows. Then she pulled the power lever over even farther and gave a hoarse order.

"On the floor, the lot of you! Cover your eyes and hope for the best."

Instantly they all flung themselves flat, and were held there by the terrific pace the Ultra was making. They waited through agonizing seconds, their eyes closed and their arms flung over them. They wondered if after all they had hit the wrong type of rock and lost their 'flashpoint,' so long did the waiting seem. Then, it came!

For a second a brilliance beyond imagination blasted through the purple window shields, through the upflung arms, through the tightly closed eyelids. Brief though it was, there was surely nothing so incredibly effulgent than the instant release of trillions of ergs of energy in one mighty burst.

The five hung on to themselves, breathing hard, perspiration rolling down their faces and spots of green light bouncing before their tortured eyes, Then, gradually, the Amazon dared to lift her head.

Blazing sunlight was pouring through the window shields. The control room was as hot as the edge of Hades as, outside, a mighty ball of uncontrollable atomic fire came to the zenith. So much the Amazon glimpsed, then she lowered her head again and closed her eyes against the light.

Minutes passed. She looked again. The glare was less. More minutes, as the Ultra winged its way at almost the speed of light through infinite space. On and on, its velocity ever increasing, until at last the control room was gloomily dark—dark, that is, by comparison with the unbearable light of the earlier moments. Only then did the Amazon stir, and the others with her.

She crossed to the switchboard and pressed the button that allowed the purple shields to fly back into place. Silently the five gazed on to the eternal void. They beheld a large, first-magnitude star, alone in its grandeur, a true sun, to be kindled for unguessable ages to come by drifting atomic dust in the cosmos, tides of radiation, and all those other mystic energies with which the Almighty sees fit to feed his monsters of flame, heat, and life.

"Well, we did it," the Amazon said quietly, at last, looking back. "In less than an hour that star will be a pinpoint, at our present speed. In two hours it will be as though it had never existed. The adventure's finished with, and if you ask me, a job well done."

There was silence for a moment, then Thania said slowly: "Yes, we've finished with that adventure, but maybe we've flown into another one."

"Another one?" The Amazon stared at her. "But—in what way?"

For answer, the teenager nodded through the window. The others could not determine at first what she meant. Then suddenly they all became aware of something moving infinitely far ahead among the stars.

"What is it?" Mexone asked, puzzled. "At this distance, I'd say it's a large-sized spaceship. Not that there's anything unusual about that. A spaceship could easily be on its way from a distant planet and we've crossed its path."

Viona moved across to the telescope, swung it on its bearings, then focused it. She gave a whistle of amazement.

"If this doesn't beat everything!" she exclaimed. "Thania's right. We're definitely on the edge of something new."

"Why? What's wrong?" the Amazon demanded.

"There's a mystery here!" Viona looked up excitedly. "Believe it or not, that distant spaceship is the Ultra! In every detail, even to the name on the prow. Come and look for yourselves!"

One by one the others did so, only to confirm Viona's statement for themselves.

"Definitely a duplicate of the Ultra," the Amazon agreed. "And since we've never been in this region of space before, I don't see how it could happen."

"But evidently it has," Abna said, moving to the control board. "And the sooner we find out what's happened, the better."

He shifted the power lever, then glanced back at the others.

"Hang on to yourselves, everybody! The Ultra is going to meet the Ultra—and soon!"

AUTHOR'S PREFACE TO "BLACK EMPRESS"

Reprinted from John Russell Fearn's article in the "Meet the Authors" feature of the January 1939 issue of Amazing Stories, *in which this story first appeared.*

* * * *

Black Empress is an endeavor to conform to the standard of *Amazing* to produce both an adventurous scientific story with a human interest. The mysterious transformation of a girl one might meet in any walk of life into a ruthless killer, is, I believe, a situation a man might meet up with in the scientific age that lies ahead of us—and to that end I have tried to depict the reasons for the change, and the possibilities that might lie ahead of any one of us.

To write of this story without giving away the solution is rather difficult, but most of it is, I think, based on possible facts. Again, it struck me when plotting the story that bearded old men usually seem responsible for the world's tragedies and uplifts (in the scientific yarns of the old school anyway) so I supplied a fresh twist in having a woman do the trick for a change.

The transformation of all forms of life; the segregation of labor and capital, would be almost bound to follow such a ruthless conquest as here. That, too, I have tried to convey.

I believe indeed, and always have, that we move about among forces such as I have described. How are we to know that each one of us is private unto himself? I do not think so. I believe that the cosmos has minds that have already studied us in every detail—that the things that happened to Madge Cromwell could happen to any one of us—only with this possible difference. Super minds may not consider us worth the trouble of experimentation. Can you blame them? When we attain to the realm of pure intelligence, then maybe we will know what these mind forces are that are eternally grouped, unseen around us.

BLACK EMPRESS

CHAPTER I

A Meteor

Doctor Asa Cromwell's extraordinary scientific knowledge and deep-rooted fear of war certainly led his genius into strange channels. When the war scare of was rife, when it seemed inevitable that nation would rise relentlessly against nation, he turned his far-reaching intelligence to the devising of machinery for the immediate protection of his own home, the extensive land he owned, and, if they'd have it, his country.

Living some miles outside Trenton he was definitely free of the bustle and disturbance of city life. His home was a detached one with laboratory annexed, wherein he worked steadily, aided by his wife until she died unexpectedly. At that time, however, his daughter Madge was well old enough to understand most of the science on which she had been quite willingly nurtured. Having more than a natural taste for things scientific, loving her father heart and soul, she made him a perfect assistant. They went on laboring together as the years passed.

Ironically enough the war scare had ceased then. Peace was being talked all over the world. And therefore Dr. Cromwell's brilliant inventions, when he tried to sell them, were practically of no value.

About this time young Edward Melton dropped into the scene. Refreshingly impudent, blond headed and square jawed, he made no secret of the fact that he enjoyed his job as a traveler in metals, covering one end of America to the other in a smooth running sedan.

It was an order for tungsten alloy of a special grade that brought him to the massive, solitary Cromwell residence.

The Doctor himself was brief, curt as the very devil in fact, and Ted Melton for once wished tungsten alloy was not in his line. Then he caught sight of Madge and had a brief talk with her. From then on his interest in tungsten alloy was enormous... And so he gradually merged, in what spare time he had, into being a part of the Cromwell setup.

When his travels brought him near Trenton he spent the time with raven headed, white skinned Madge at every opportunity—that was when he could get rid of Cromwell, whose eye for romance had gone blind long ago.

"Think of it!" cried Cromwell, one night. "This spot on earth, this one stretch of good American soil which I own, is utterly indestructible!" He went to the open French windows and stared out on the mellow dark of the July evening. He was an odd, bent little figure, acid stained hands clenched behind him. "I have wrought a lasting peace out of machinery," he went on slowly, half to himself. "Nothing of man's making can ever hurt me or my dear one. Here—right here—is paradise!"

"Yeah," agreed Ted laconically, and his blue eyes were intensely bored. He reflected that paradise might take several forms.

"Do you realize," Cromwell said, turning swiftly, "what I have accomplished?" He came back into the comfortable room with a certain challenge, pointing his toes as he walked. As ever, his lean, clever face was massed into a thousand wrinkles of concentration; his high brow was furrowed, his gray hair awry.

"I have mastered the forces of the atom, I have created energy shields that can deflect the mightiest bomb ever made, I have created molecular disrupters that can shift matter itself—can destroy a building of steel in five minutes. I could, if I chose, be master of the world," he finished softly.

Madge laughed a little. "Oh, dad, don't be so absurd!" she rebuked him. "Master the world! What good would it do you?"

"None, I suppose," he confessed; then added with a grim frown, "I could, just the same. The machines I have got..."

"Say, I smell something!" Ted interrupted suddenly, sitting

erect and sniffing. "Smells like water spilled on a fire."

Cromwell started. "Good Lord, my beaker!" he gasped. "I'd quite forgotten it…"

He went out of the French windows at a run, vanished over the dark garden to the lighted expanse of laboratory. Ted grinned faintly as he looked at the girl.

"Grand old dear, isn't he?" he murmured.

The girl's straight, sensitive features were just a trifle drawn in sudden anxiety.

"The best in the world," she answered slowly, "but sometimes, Ted, I feel sorry for him. He's spent all his life making these engines of destruction—" she sighed heavily—"and now there's no need of them. At heart he's embittered; I know it. He's been that way ever since mother died. Sometimes I wonder…"

She stopped, looked round with concerned dark eyes.

"Wonder what?" Ted prompted gently.

"If his natural pride will get the better of him one day. Believe me, Ted, his talk about world mastery is horribly true—that's why I laugh it off. If he really became serious about it—even I could do it if I was so minded."

"Huh? Good Heavens, you're not implying—"

"Of course not," she smiled. "You know me better than that… Besides, I've got you now. I've pretty well finished helping dad. We're engaged—in two months we'll be married. What would I want with such inventions, anyhow? It was different when war was such a grim danger. My only worry is that dad, left to himself, brooding constantly over those machines, might do something really dangerous."

"Needless worry, I'm sure," Ted said quietly. "A man of his genius has got all the balance necessary, don't you forget it. He won't go off half-cocked. Besides, we'll keep looking in on him to see he's all right and— Look!" he broke off suddenly with a hoarse cry, and his hand darted upwards to point through the French windows.

The girl looked up just in time to see a blinding streak of fire blaze across the heavens. The scream of tortured air sounded like an express train roaring out of emptiness. For an instant the grounds of the house, the immense adjoining laboratory, the whole land-scape beyond, were flooded in brilliant green radiance—then the monster meteorite had dropped over the western horizon.

There was a dull, remote concussion, the faint shaking of the ground that made loose articles give a momentary rattle... Then darkness and stillness had returned.

"Gosh, what a meteor!" Ted managed to gasp out at length. "I wonder where it dropped?"

The girl had risen to her feet. "Didn't seem very far from Norristown to me. If it really did drop there..." She left her sentence unfinished as her father came tearing in from the garden.

"Did you see it?" he gasped hoarsely. "About the biggest thing since the Siberian meteorite. I was standing at the lab window as it went over us."

"Hardly as big as the Siberian meteorite, dad," Madge corrected gently. "Pretty large, yes, but don't forget the actual size would be smaller. The expanding halo of gas around it caused by the friction of—"

"Don't try and teach me science, young woman!" the scientist broke in curtly. Then he strode vigorously across to the newscasting machine and switched it on.

The New York relay station had no intimation of the occurrence neither bad Trenton. Impatiently Cromwell switched over to the Philadelphia relay. For a while there was nothing unusual, then the cold mechanical voice, synthetically created, spoke deliberately.

"A meteorite, measuring twelve feet in diameter or thereabouts, spherical in form, has dropped a few miles east of Pottstown and buried itself in a crater roughly approximated at eight feet in depth. Fortunately little serious damage has been caused. The particular area where it fell is pastureland, the main damage being to crops. The glare was seen as jar east as Mid Atlantic and as far west as Los Angeles. Investigation will commence when the meteorite has cooled..."

"Huh!" Cromwell switched off impatiently. "Is that all? Just another chunk or iron out of space. Why doesn't something exciting happen?" he demanded. "Why couldn't it have dropped near here?"

"And choked us with superheated gas?" Madge asked pointedly. "Hang it all, dad! Good job it fell where it did, if you ask me."

"Make a note!" her father ordered briefly. "It'll take about three days for the meteorite to cool completely; then we'll go and examine it. May be interesting…"

He went out slowly as the girl nodded assent. Ted turned to her.

"Well, I guess our thrill fell flat," he sighed. "Pity…" He glanced at his watch. "Well, I'll have to be going. I'm on a tour that'll take me to Bridgeport and New Haven tomorrow, so for a month at least we'll be separated. I'm making my base in New York, so I can be in touch with the firm. You can find me at the Grand Western Hotel…"

"I'll remember," the girl smiled, as he kissed her gently.

CHAPTER II

A Strange Death

Absorbed by the unusually busy spell which ensued during the next few days, Ted had little chance to think much of Madge, though he did read in the papers and hear over the public newscasters that parties of scientists. Madge and her father among them, had visited the fallen meteorite upon its cooling, discovered that it was not the conventional nickel iron affair, but composed of a metal of tremendously high fusing point.

In fact, the fuse point was so high there was nothing in earthly science that could even make a dent on the cooled metal.

Scientific institutes and museums began to bid against each other for the possession of the object. The former wanted to study it; the latter to have it as souvenir. The New York Museum of Natural History won, backed by public opinion. In the Museum the thing could be seen by an interested populace; in the scientific institutes it would just vanish from sight. And, on being transported to New York, the thing was further rendered a mystery by being far lighter than its mass suggested—unless as one observer suggested, it was really hollow…

Telephoning Madge, Ted learned that old man Cromwell was deeply annoyed because he couldn't get a piece of the meteorite to study. Besides, his bitterest rival in the scientific world—Justin Cavil—had openly laughed at him. Nothing was more calculated to make Asa Cromwell burn… So now, according to the girl, he was working feverishly on ways and means of destroying impregnable metal, pottering around in his laboratory day and night.

A few more days of traveling, bargaining and buying, then Ted returned to his New York hotel one evening to meet up with a surprise. Madge was seated waiting for him, her face drawn and strained, her big dark eyes enlarged and red from weeping.

"Why, Madge dearest, what on earth—?" Instantly Ted was at her side, soothing her gently as she burst into another fit of crying. He took her slim shoulders rather roughly, forced her to look at him. For the first time he noticed that she was all in black.

"What is it, honey?" he murmured. "Don't cry—please! You can tell me. Is it—your father?" he asked slowly.

Madge nodded bitterly, her lower lip quivering.

"He's—he's dead, Ted. Heart failure— Or anyway that's what the doctor said. Somehow I can't believe it..." She broke off, twisting her damp handkerchief; forced herself to be calm. "Oh, I haven't known what I've been doing the last few days," she muttered. "Such a whirl! I tried to get you here, but they told me you were away for a couple of days—"

"I'm sorry," he said quietly. "Business kept me away from New York. Please go on..."

"Dad died—died three days ago, the day after you telephoned me. It was late in the evening, nearly dark. I was in the library and I heard a sudden scream from the laboratory. French window§ were open. When I got to dad he—he was dead. Buried him today then... Then I came to find you."

She sank her dark head on Ted's shoulder. His arm embraced her shoulders again.

"O.K., take it easy," he soothed. "These things have got to happen, you know—will go on happening until science finds a way to defeat death... Funny, though, him dying of heart failure like that. Didn't strike me as that sort of a man."

"There are so many things I don't understand," the girl mumbled. "The lab was all upset, just as though there'd been a fight of some sort. A heavy instrument stand was overturned too—so heavy I couldn't lift it up. I don't know how dad's slight form came to knock it over— Oh, I don't know what to think!"

"Was anything stolen?" Ted asked sharply.

"Not a thing; that's the queer part. And since dad was dead he couldn't tell anything, of course. Still, the doctor said heart failure, probably brought on by extreme shock."

"Odd... Damned odd," Ted muttered. "What a pity you didn't think of taking an ultra violet photograph of his eyes after death; the retinae would have retained the last image for quite a little time."

"I did," she sighed. "It was a horrible job—and fruitless. It only showed a vision of me in the doorway, which was quite natural. Dad couldn't have been quite dead as I entered—died a second or two afterwards..." She shrugged and relapsed into moody silence.

Ted scratched his blond head rather helplessly. "Well, I guess there's nothing I can say. To offer sympathy is so darned conventional. Is everything well locked up at home?"

"With all the combination locks," the girl answered, trying hard to smile. "You remember how impregnable dad made his laboratory. It's safe enough. As for me, I've got the room next door, complete with my trunk and bags. I'm staying here for the rest of the month until you're through with your job, then we can go back to Trenton and decide what to do."

"We'll get married, that's what," he answered firmly. "And now, young lady, you're corning downstairs to have a good meal."

* * * *

Madge duly domiciled herself in the Grand Western Hotel and tried as best she could to overcome her grief. By the following morning she had herself much better in hand, was almost cheerful as Ted left her.

When he returned in the evening he received a tremendous shock

Madge had gone—completely! There was nothing mysterious about her actual departure; the riddle was her reason for doing so. The reception clerk laconically observed that she had checked out during the afternoon, taken away the luggage she had brought the previous evening, and had left no forwarding address.

Ted was simply dumbfounded. It did not make sense for her to walk out like this without a single word of explanation. Harassedly he tried to think of something he had said to offend her, but he could only recollect her gentle kiss in the morning, her smiling promise to look forward to his return.

From the moment he left the reception clerk Ted lost all sense of time, went in and out of the telephone booth almost continuously, ringing up the Trenton house—Always the same sing-song response—"No reply, I'm sorry."

He tackled the commissionaire and was referred to the taxi drivers. Here he got hold of one clue, at least. One driver had taken the girl to the Pennsylvania Railroad Station. Immediately Ted went there and pestered officials and booking clerks, but they couldn't help him. He didn't even know what clothes she had been wearing. She might have taken any train anywhere. The thing was utterly hopeless.

From the station he again telephoned Trenton. Still no answer. Desperate, he got out his car and streaked through the night, reached the great residence some time after midnight and found it locked and deserted. The girl was certainly not there; had vanished as completely as if into thin air.

Into the morning of the next day he worried police and detective bureaus, did all in his power without finding any further clues. Finally there was nothing for it but to leave things to the police. Exhausted, unutterably miserable, he returned to his New York hotel and went straight to bed, worn out.

Ted abandoned work, abandoned everything in the weeks that ensued, spent all his time, day in and day out, trying to locate Madge. His hard earned savings began to deplete alarmingly.

In a month he was a ghost of his former hale and hearty self— was unshaven, baffled, badly groomed. Certain tacit observations by the hotel management jerked him into a sense of decency and he took himself in hand. Then one evening, as he sat puzzling in his room, the telephone bell rang sharply.

Wearily he lifted the receiver.

"Ted?" came a familiar voice. "Oh, Ted, thank God it's you!"

"Madge!" he yelled, leaping up. "Madge darling, where are you? What in Heaven's name is all this about?" His fingers dug hard into the receiver.

The girl's voice was tense and low pitched, clearly nervous.

"Ted, come to me!" she implored desperately. "I think I'm going mad! It's awful! I'm at home, and—"

Her voice stopped abruptly, her sentence ending in a low gasp. There was a click, then the line went dead.

Ted slammed the telephone down, and went downstairs like a whirlwind. Within seconds he'd gotten his car from the garage, within minutes he was in the thick of the New York traffic.

He drove resolutely through the night and reached the Trenton residence around 1:30 in the morning. It stood in dark isolation against the moon, unlighted, apparently still deserted. Ignoring these evidences he raced to the front door and slammed heavily on the knocker, punched the bell, waited anxiously as there was no answer.

Then to his intense relief lights came up in the hall—he heard footsteps. The door opened gradually and Madge's slim, smoothly rounded figure was silhouetted against the streaming glare.

"Madge!" he cried thankfully, strode forward and crushed her slender body in his arms, smothered her face in kisses. "Oh, darling, thank God I found you again!"

He broke off and looked at the girl in surprise as she very deliberately pushed him away from her. Her lovely face was set, curiously hard.

"Don't, Ted—please!" she ordered quietly. "That sort of thing is all finished with. Everything's finished—between us."

Ted stared at her, could find no words to say. She was smiling a little now, an aloof coldly cynical smile that looked foreign on her sensitive mouth.

"I've come to a decision," she went on steadily. "In fact I came to it that day when I walked out of the hotel. I suddenly saw myself for an absolute fool! The whole world at my feet and nothing being done about it! A laboratory full of stuff to bend humanity to my will, and I just let it lie there and rot. Dad died giving his all to those inventions. The least I can do is to use them!"

"But—but dearest, I can't believe my ears!" Ted stammered, staring at her in the bright light. "You sound like a different woman entirely. We were going to be married…"

"Marriage!" Her lips were scornful. "Good Heavens, Ted, that is out of the question. Maybe it was dad's death that brought me to my senses."

"Or else drove you out of them!" Ted retorted, flushing hotly. He suddenly seized the gir¾s silk clad arms in an iron grip, shook her fiercely. "What's all this about?" he snapped. "For one thing, what are you doing fully dressed at this hour in the morning?"

"Any objections?" she asked icily, jerking her arms free. "I'm checking over the resources of the laboratory. In a couple of days—maybe sooner—I'll put my plans into action."

"But your phone call!" Ted burst out frantically. "You said you needed me, then broke off suddenly with a sort of gasp."

She shrugged. "Guess you're right. Just for a while I wavered in my intentions, was weak enough to send for you. You must have imagined the gasp. I only rang off because I realized what a fool I was making of myself when I've otherwise gotten everything so nicely in hand."

"I see." Ted studied her cold gaze and felt himself tingle with a sudden desire to slap her violently in the face.

Why that idea got hold of him he did not know. He was only conscious of an intense change of feeling toward this now cold, statuesque woman to whom his heart had been given.

"Listen, Madge," he said thickly; "you don't realize what you're walking into! A life of massacre and crime—that's what it amounts to. You can't do it! I won't let you do it! You're unhinged or something through the death of your father—I'm going to stop you!" he finished desperately.

Her dark head shook. "No you're not, Ted. Nobody's going to stop me, because nobody *can* stop me! You should know that by this time!"

"But, Madge—"

"Get out!" she commanded bitterly, and he stared back in amazement as her white hand reached momentarily into a sash about her waist and produced a gleaming revolver.

"And remember," she resumed grimly, her lips hard and set, "I'll not have you around me any more. Whatever there was between us is finished now. The old sniveling Madge Cromwell is dead; instead there remains the future conqueror of the world. The only woman in history to master a planet. Now—go!"

Too confused to think straight Ted backed to the door, the girl's queenly form following him up relentlessly. His last vision of her was her unwavering automatic, the cold stare of her dark eyes, then the door closed in his face and he was out in the cool night wind.

CHAPTER III

Empress of the Earth

Three days later, at eleven in the morning, a neutral airplane of bombing dimensions—neutral in so far that it bore no insignia—was sighted at 5,000 feet over Central Park. Aeronautical experts were interested, but puzzled. The plane had no right there, was directly out of the ordinary trade and passenger lines, and since planes were required by law to be identified the matter was distinctly a mystery to officials.

Sky police patrols set off to question the flyer—only to discover that the machine turned tail and flew at unbelievable speed westwards. The police patrol returned to earth.

Then at three in the afternoon the mystery plane returned, circling slowly in ominous wide sweeps, directly over the dead center of Madison Square. Its silence was disquieting.

People stared up at it with shaded eyes; the airway bureaus got busy again. Then all New York was stunned o into amazement by the sight of four investigating police planes crumbling to pieces in mid-air! Nothing was visible near the stationary interloper, no rays of any kind, yet as the police patrol swept forward they smashed into atoms at a distance of five hundred feet from the strange plane, dropped in flaming ruins on the metropolis below. The possibility of invasion flashed across the minds of the people. The vessel still circled slowly. Then from the newscasters there suddenly burst a howl of interference, wiping out the intoned news of the hour. A woman's voice, slow and measured, spoke.

"People, I am Madge Cromwell. An ordinary name, but remember that Asa Cromwell was my father, and the greatest scientific genius of this age. He invented armaments for your safety, which you refused; he went to the very ends of scientific research so that you might have peace and security. You refused it! There can only be one answer to such dolts. The weapons that could have protected you will be turned against you! I make no demands, no ultimatum, I demand no particular obedience because in the end that will be an easy thing to obtain. Those of you who wish to come to my side after I have proved my powers may signify that fact by gathering in the desert regions of Arizona. You will then receive further instructions. I have power—infinite power, and shall use it. Watch!"

The voice ceased. The monster air machine suddenly moved to one side, darted like a striking eagle to the north and circled again between Wall Street and Broadway. People below, drawn by that radio communication, stood watching open-mouthed—then something happened.

A pale violet beam stabbed from the bottom of the vessel, swept ruthlessly over the buildings that imprisoned Wall Street. In an instant the canyon of finance was a mass of flying bricks, shorn off steel girders and crumbling glass. Whole tops lifted off buildings like built up cards scattering in a wind—came shattering down on the screaming, running populace below.

Madge Cromwell had struck the first blow—and it was only the beginning.

As the frantic people stormed and swept in the debris littered streets, as ambulances flew desperately to the grim scene, the big plane swept onwards on its tour of destruction. Nothing seemed able to withstand that relentless beam.

Broadway was the next to be attacked. Huge, smoking holes were torn in solid concrete, buildings caved inwards, subways sloughed and shattered into the depths and imprisoned those underground. Then onward to the harbors and docks where the sea boiled under the impact of the beam and ships vomited skywards in a million pieces under its inconceivable power.

Back again up the river, and Brooklyn, Manhattan and Williamsburgh Bridge went one after the other, left behind a story of inhuman massacre and destruction.

In the course of that ghastly afternoon over 20,000 people died, and twice the number were seriously injured by flying splinters and collapsing buildings.

Madge Cromwell had declared merciless war—a war that enraged America was eager to fight. Entire armadas of attackers started off in pursuit of the bomber as it zig-zagged on a trail of destruction which incorporated Long Island, Fifth Avenue, the destruction of the Empire State Building, the wrecking of Central Park, and the smashing of George Washington Bridge into fused and twisted girders.

The avenging fighters swept with ruthless savagery on the black invader, but they suffered the same fate as the police patrol. Every machine within five hundred feet of the invader crumpled up as though hurled into a steel wall at hundreds of miles an hour. They shattered down and added their load of fire and ruin to the chaos below.

With a calm ruthlessness that was terrifying the killer plane's beam lifted for a moment from the destruction below and turned its attention to the attacking squadrons. They were simply sliced out of being, cut in half, blown into thin air. Bullets, missiles, anti-aircraft guns—they made not the least effect on the strange plane.

Madge Cromwell's ship apparently was using an energy shell, generated from the atomic power of copper and radiated into a perfect shield at 500 ft. radius, keeping the plane protected with a force a thousand times stronger than steel itself—a mesh of repulsive energy that no possible form of matter or explosion could penetrate.

The beam seemed to be a ramification of the same thing—an intra-atomic wave, concentrated down an electromagnetic beam and utterly shattering molecular structure by shifting entire atoms out of their orbits.

At five hundred feet every attack was deflected, and for retaliation instant searing death rained down on the defenders.

And Madge Cromwell was behind it all! Ted went sick at the very thought of it. All the love he had ever had for her turned to burning hate. This senseless, inhuman slaughter; the screaming from the street outside the so far untouched hotel, the thunder of explosions as edifice after edifice was slashed out of being.

He rather wondered about the airplane itself. He had never seen it before and presumed it must be an ordinary fast bomber equipped by Madge.

Towards evening the plane departed westward with its usual terrific speed, pursued until it outdistanced the defending planes.

By now the whole country was ready. Planes were everywhere. They came from every city and coastline, pursued the invader until the late evening—according to the newscasters. Then at nightfall it was lost, due mainly to silencers on its engine, which defied all powers of penetration. Ted, helping in the streets with the wounded, guessed it had dropped down to the impenetrable laboratory where it was just as untouchable as in the air, surrounded by an area of force.

He resolved more than ever to keep himself out of the trouble. If he revealed the site of the laboratory he would probably be suspected as an accessory—and anyway the world knew where Asa Cromwell had lived and would invade the spot soon enough.

By midnight, America was declared to be at war. All war measures were put into force—nor was America alone. The inhuman nature of the attack had aroused the ire of other nations. Great Britain offered her immediate aid—and her Commonwealth. Canada, in particular, marched into action. Europe arose, too, ready to strike down the invader before any attack could be made. It seemed that in the space of twelve hours the whole world turned upside down...but that was only the beginning.

Ted was one of the first to join up, though he pretty well knew the futility of it. Madge Cromwell struck for increasingly long periods in the days that followed, swept back and forth across America. One by one cities were reduced to shambles of ruin and flame. Chicago, Pittsburgh, Philadelphia, Los Angeles, Columbus—one after the other they smashed down under the violet beam. Hundreds upon hundreds of planes, incalculable numbers of missiles and shells were rained through the skies—with no more effect than flirting peas at an elephant. The Black Empress, as Madge Cromwell had come to be known, was indestructible.

In two weeks of absolutely unchecked ferocity she had destroyed nearly all the civilization of America. Then she was not seen for weeks on end, but there came news of destruction of London, Berlin, Leningrad, Stockholm, Paris and Sydney; all over the world she had the upper hand. Nowhere else was there anybody who understood the devastating power of unleashed atomic force: even if there was there was no time to invent a counter weapon. Suddenness and ruthlessness were the perfect weapons of victory.

Slowly but surely the morale of the defenders and harassed people began to weaken. In America, countless thousands trekked over the shattered country to the open deserts of Arizona, there to camp in signification of their willingness to obey the merciless destroyer.

In other countries various places were assigned by Madge Cromwell for volunteer followers of her rule—and little by little she had her way. Her very invulnerability gave her the victory. In six weeks she had won.

Ted Melton was one of those who fought to the last with an anti-aircraft squad in shattered New York. Bemused and bewildered, utterly exhausted from long hours of struggle without any sign of proper morale, he could hardly believe it when he realized that the short, one-sided war was over—that the girl he had loved was mistress of the situation.

He wanted to rise from the litter of dust and shattered bodies to curse the very skies, rain blasphemies on the Creator that had ever permitted her to be born. Millions of innocent lives destroyed—to please one woman with an ambition to rule the Earth. And would that alone suffice?

Ted sighed, moved out of the hot, festering hole where he had nursed the gun, joined others in their tin hats from under which leered grim, dirty faces.

"Heard the news?" asked one of them, briefly.

"That the woman's won? Yeah," Ted acknowledged bitterly.

"That isn't all," the man said, glaring around him in the twilight. "We've got to stop around this muckheap of a city until we're picked up. We're to be detailed or somethin'. I guess the Black Empress is going to give her favors to them yellow bellies who went to Arizona—those who were so darned afraid of her they gave up fighting. Hell!" The man spat thickly to illustrate his venom. "Blast her very name!" he finished acridly.

CHAPTER IV

Two Years Later

Ted Melton became one of a roving band of people, finding food where he could, sleeping where he could, a hungry and embittered being hating everybody and everything.

He had not so much hatred for Madge Cromwell now; more a kind of numbness when he thought of her and saw on every hand the sufferings she had caused. Again and again he cursed himself as a yellow coward for not having killed her that night when he'd had the chance. He could have risked her automatic.

But it was no use now. Two years had passed. Nothing to do but drag on, endlessly, he knew not where, through a land where happiness and progress had gone. He presumed the rest of the world was the same.

He wandered onwards through another chilly Fall, braved the blizzards of a third winter in a small camp. Men and women were persistently with him, their faces set and haggard, filled with frozen hate. Some of the fiercer spirits slew every woman they came across because of her very sex. Along the waysides dead women, horribly mutilated, were by no means uncommon. The name of Madge Cromwell, the Black Empress, was spurned and reviled to the ends of the earth.

Bearded, keeping to himself as much as he could, Ted was just a wandering nonentity. Until one day in the early summer of the following year, when wandering through uncultured fields near former Chicago, he and his colleagues came face to face with a band of uniformed guards—tall, powerful men, armed with objects that looked like glorified lead pencils. In this resemblance their harmlessness ended.

They projected a beam identical, on a small scale, to the one with which Madge Cromwell had mastered the Earth.

The sullen party waited as the men came up. In silence Ted studied the insignia on their sleeves, together with the two letters—

B. E. Black Empress, presumably. He smiled a little twistedly.

"Names!" snapped the leader of the party, and wrote them down as they were given. He cast pale blue eyes over the tattered group, gave a sharp order and had them bundled into a waiting truck.

Ted was not particularly concerned where he went. In any case his view was limited to a small barred window. Ever and again the truck stopped and picked up more fugitives, then rumbled on. It seemed to travel forever across tangled countryside. No halts, no food or water, onward into the night with the women and children crying softly and the men muttering oaths in their beards.

Endless miles it seemed.

Ted found himself dozing—was next awakened in the cold light of dawn by a rough hand pulling his shoulder.

Stupidly he fell outside and shivered in the cool wind.

"Where—where are we?" he mumbled, staring round on the towering buildings.

The uniformed guard grinned a little mirthlessly. "It's New York. Not the one that used to be here—the new one. See that over there"—he pointed to a slender tower rising over all the other buildings; "that's her abode."

"The Black Empress'?" Ted asked dully, staring at the dawn light smiting its topmost heights.

"Yeah. She's ruler of the world now, you know. She's gotten machines in that tower as tough as those she conquered us with. I don't like her any more than you do, only I slid into a good job as a guard so I'm not grumbling. Besides, what's the use of arguing with a death ray? I guess you'll be one of the workers—like those that built the city. All different now, you know. We're rounding up the outsiders in the countryside—all over the world in fact. Getting things shipshape again. Now let's go, folks."

He turned, followed by the people, while in the rear the other guards came up silently. Pawns, all of them—captors and captured.

* * * *

The morning passed within an enormous building with heavily barred windows, evidently the prison. Ted and numberless other fugitives were fed and allowed to wash—then in mid-afternoon he was taken with the others to the girl's headquarters, taken up to the lofty top floor in the elevator and ushered into a room that blazed with lights.

It reminded him of a criminal scanning room of the old days. Guards were everywhere. Against the lighted wall height-lines were drawn. An automatic measuring machine made an absolute check of each person's size as they filed into the glare, stood silent, and waited while a calm, measured voice pronounced exactly what duty they were to fulfil.

Ted listened to the voice in grim silence—it was Madge's. He'd know it anywhere, save that its soft sweetness was entirely absent. It was the all conquering voice of a world ruler.

He listened to the monotonous detailing of instructions, gathered that the girl could see everything that was going on from an adjoining room. Some of the assignments she gave rather puzzled him. Underground workers? Extraction Plants? Blast cannon units?

They made no sense to him.

Then it came his turn. Along with the others his name was read out. Immediately the voice ordered him to stand aside. He waited under guard until every other person had been assigned a task, then he was touched on the shoulder and led into an adjoining room—a vast office, wide and imposing, severely but sensibly furnished and backed with a great window which commanded an entire view of the new and still embryonic New York City

His gaze passed over the steel doors that presumably hid the devilish machinery chambers, to the great desk studded with various buttons, and so to the slim still girlish figure standing by the desk itself. The streaming sunshine caught the soft curves of her figure, the raven black of her hair.

"Come in, Ted." Her voice was like finely tempered steel. He came forward slowly, staring at her with somber, smoldering eyes. A slow, cruel smile curved her fine lips, made her teeth shine in the flood of light.

"Rather a long interval between meetings, isn't it?" she asked lightly, straightening up. "But you see, I kept my word. I have conquered the world."

"I know." Ted's voice was low, dispassionate. "And what's it gotten you? What man, woman or child is there in the world who doesn't hate you? God, Madge, if I'd ever even thought— The things you have to answer for!" he finished in awed horror.

"Sentiment," she said slowly, "never did mix with science. I learned that when I decided to use father's inventions. It was quite exciting while it lasted—particularly as I was, and still am, invulnerable."

"You can destroy life as heartlessly as that?" Ted whispered. "It's—it's just a game?"

Her shoulders shrugged; she was still smiling unconcernedly.

"Absolute power brings freedom of thought, Ted," she observed. "I know I'm the Empress and now I'm going to put certain plans into effect. Control of the world is not enough; I intend to go further—conquer space. I believe I can from what dad told me."

Ted stepped forward to directly face her. "In God's name, Madge, what is the matter with you?" he panted. "Am I mad, or are you? Is all this some terrible dream from which I'll awake to find the old, lovable Madge I wanted to marry, or does it mean that you are the greatest murderess in Earth's history?"

"In the process of advancement from the grosser forms of existence millions are bound to die," she answered thoughtfully. "I gave everybody the chance of obeying me. Those that refused deserved to die."

"There's nothing too terrible for your punishment," Ted whispered, staring at her dark, level eyes. "Nothing!"

She laughed cynically. "I have heard various suggestions for my disposal—strangling, crucifixion, burning at the stake. All of which is very amusing because I hold the master key. I can't be beaten."

"Until I'm dead, Madge, I'll never rest until you are beaten! I'll dedicate my life to it—to your destruction instead of to our happiness. I'll get you one day, even if I have to come crawling back from the grave to do it!"

"Melodrama—and cheap melodrama too!" she flared at him, her slender body taut in sudden fury. "You driveling fool, Ted! What chance do you stand? Why do you think I brought you in here? To beg your forgiveness? Oh, no! Our association ended way back in Trenton. I brought you here to have a fresh look at you and to show you that I've kept my promise to rule the world. Also, I shall assign you to work."

She paused and considered. "Maybe you heard some of the

other assignments?"

"Extraction Plants? Blast cannons? Yes, I heard them," he assented grimly. "I didn't get their meaning, all the same."

"You will, some day." She smiled twistedly. "In the meantime, it might be a good idea to have you work in one of the cannon shafts. No—no, a better plan! In one of the Extraction Plants! It's a nice hard job, connected with extraction of chlorophyll from vegetation."

Ted stared. "Chlorophyll?" he echoed. "What the devil do you want that for?"

"That's my business!" she retorted. She turned and pressed a desk button; a uniformed guard came in and saluted.

"Detail Five!" she snapped. "Extraction Plant. That's all."

The man saluted again and Ted found his arm seized. The girl's cynical eyes followed him as he left the room; they were the last vision he had of her as the door closed— Or at least almost the last vision. As he waited in the hall while other men and women were gathered together he caught sight of the girl again, half an hour later, in the private elevator.

He stared frozenly across at her as she looked at him through the little glass window. Then to his amazement he saw her dark eyes fill suddenly with tears; her lower lip quivered—

Then the elevator rose upwards and carried her out of sight.

Tears? After all she had said and done to him? Ted began to believe he really was mad, that the things that were happening were part of a delirium.

CHAPTER V

Justin Cavil—Scientist

The site of the Extraction Plant, covering several square miles, was situated on what had formerly been New York's East side. Now all traces of the old had been removed—instead, fronting all along the new harbors and docks, were numberless roofs of the same height, quickly constructed and rather shoddy buildings, laid out with a certain coldly methodical efficiency.

It reminded Ted, as they approached the site in the truck, of a vast group of barracks or a tremendous penitentiary.

"Guess you're right at that," agreed one of his fellow prisoners. "The actual Extraction Plant is a mile northward; these buildings are where the workers live. Charming, isn't it?" His lip curled bitterly. "Absolute freedom so far as it goes, yet if we set foot beyond the boundary of this little colony we'll be shot down."

The man relapsed into silence and Ted kept himself company with his own thoughts until he finally tumbled from the truck and was allotted Billet 7 in the colony. The place was not so bad—there was every needful convenience on a small scale. Except for the grim suggestion of prison life he had no particular kick.

He and his colleagues were divided up, given the rest of the day to accustom themselves to the new surroundings and were warned to stand by for work on the morrow.

Just after nightfall Ted was surprised to see his billet door open and an elderly man in overalls came in. As he took off his hat he revealed a mass of white hair and lofty brow. Coming forward, the swinging light revealed dark, deep-set eyes and a pouting but determined mouth.

"Hello!" he exclaimed cordially, extending his hand. "I'm Justin Cavil. I guess you're my new billet mate, eh? They told me to expect somebody today. Glad to know you."

Ted shook hands warmly, frowned a little. "Did—did you say Justin Cavil?"

"That's right." The man's eyes twinkled. "Any objections?"

"None at all, only the name's familiar. Wish I could think where I've heard it before."

Cavil shrugged and began to lay the table from the cupboard's modest offerings.

"Extraction Plant?" he asked off-handedly.

"Yeah—start tomorrow."

"I'm there too. I'm a machine minder—except in my spare time, when I do other things."

"Such as?"

Cavil merely smiled, went on preparing the meal, maintained silence until he had the coffee to his liking. Then he sat down at the table and looked across at Ted with his serious eyes.

"Before all this happened I was a scientist," he said slowly.

"Maybe that's where you heard the name. I was a great rival of Asa Cromwell, the father of this witch who calls herself the Black Empress."

Ted started suddenly. "Good Lord, yes; I remember now! You laughed at Cromwell because he couldn't find a way to break down the Pottstown meteorite?"

"Yes, I guess that's right," the scientist chuckled. "It was all in good part, though. I tell you straight, Asa Cromwell was the cleverest scientist that ever lived, only he received more acknowledgment than I because he always got his inventions finished before me. There was nothing he created but what I created too. I have the secret of atomic power. In fact I have gone one better. I have machinery that can operate through the lower waves of matter vibration. That means a force infinitely more devastating than sub-atomic energy."

"Then—then why—?" Ted started to ask, but the old man waved him into silence.

"Why didn't I stop Madge Cromwell conquering the world?" he asked quietly. "For the simple reason that my ideas were an on paper and not in fact. There wasn't the time. But there is now!" His deep-set eyes were gleaming. "Little by little, with wires and machinery taken from the metal shops at the Extraction Plant, I am building up several machines that will defeat all the stuff Madge Cromwell has in that tower of hers. I'm saying nothing, exciting no suspicions—but I guess I'm pretty well obliged to take you into my confidence. You'd get suspicious otherwise. Not that I doubt there's a single worker would gladly help me to defeat this she-devil."

"You can count on me," Ted growled, clenching his fists.

He sat for a time in deep thought, sipping the coffee the scientist pushed towards him, then he asked slowly, "What exactly is the idea of these Extraction Plants, anyhow? What's the chlorophyll for?"

Cavil shrugged. "As yet I don't know, but I'm making plenty of guesses. All over the country where there is wood and forest land—and that includes Canada—pumping plants are being set up. At least five thousand of them are already in action. The plants drain vegetation of all its chlorophyll, which is in turn carried by pipeline to the various Extraction Plants, this one in New York here being one of a chain. In the Extraction Plants the chlorophyll is rendered absolutely one hundred percent pure; then it is passed on to another chain of factories in the open country which seal it into cylinders about four feet long and one wide.

"These go into tremendous shafts resembling cannons and are fired by the hundreds into space. Atomic force is the explosive and remote control radio from the tower guides them. And then—" Cavil shrugged. "Frankly, I don't know. I haven't found out yet where they *do* go, but it's obviously somewhere in space. Since the Empress does the remote control herself from a master switchboard in the tower it is not possible to learn anything from anybody. But I'll find out if it takes me a lifetime."

Ted wrinkled his brow. "Say, I'm not much of a scientist," he muttered, "but it does seem to me that the constant draining of chlorophyll from vegetation will deprive it of its essential use. It will affect our atmosphere if too much of it goes on. After all, any school kid knows that chlorophyll is responsible for getting rid of all toxic compounds—carbon dioxide, and so forth."

"Exactly," the scientist agreed grimly. "That is why I have to hurry—work as often as I can. For some reason this devilish woman is slowly bringing about the end of the very world she has conquered. Why? That is the mystery—which in time I will solve."

"I can't understand it," Ted muttered. "To think Madge Cromwell could turn into such a fiend…"

"That gets me too," Cavil admitted reflectively. "When I met her and her father at the site of the meteorite I was impressed by her great charm of manner. Strange indeed. Am I to understand that you know her as well?"

"I did. We were to be married, before all this."

Cavil's keen little eyes narrowed a little. "I wonder if you'd mind telling me everything?"

"Sure!" Briefly Ted outlined the general circumstances as they had happened to him, wound up with a deep sigh. "And I guess that's how it is!"

Cavil shrugged. "I'm sorry…" he said quietly. Then he got actively to his feet. "Well, I've work to get done. Maybe you'd like to see my laboratory?"

"Laboratory!" Ted gasped in wonderment. "Where?"

"Underground—about half a mile from where the old Museum

of Natural History used to be. I believe my place was originally the basement of a multiple store. Plenty of them left after the war, you know, but very few discovered. I found mine by accident. Its roof is twenty feet below ground level. Plenty of other advantages about it, too. Come along and I'll show you."

They went out together into the dull-lit regions of the workers' quarters. At the back of the little domiciles, rearing invincibly into the night sky, was the new New York, dominated by the girl's highest tower of all. Ted glanced up at it as he went slowly along, pondered its countless windows and the beacon at the extreme summit, wondered what new plans the girl was evolving.

Cavil gripped his arm.

"Down there," the scientist said, glancing swiftly around—then assured that the other workers wandering about the settlement were too far away to be suspicious, he raised a grating, dropped down into the cavity beneath. In a moment Ted was beside him, closing the grid gently. He felt around on a dry, circular wall.

"Old sewer pipe," Cavil explained. "Hang onto me."

Ted obeyed, wandered he knew not where through the low built pipe.

Then at length Cavil fumbled in his overalls for keys and undid a heavy wooden door, stepped forward and switched on a small electric light. Ted gazed in amazement on a passably well-equipped laboratory, the roof supported by heavy, crudely fixed beams for additional security.

"My hideout," the old scientist grinned. "Come right in."

He closed and locked the door.

"Bit of a comedown for a once world famous scientist," he observed, musing. "Still, no matter; those days will come back. We're safe here too."

He pointed to a door in the wall facing the entrance. "Beyond that door is a tunnel half a mile long, made by me," he said impressively. "I've dug it—little by little. And why? Because, exactly a mile and a half away from here is the Empress' tower, in a directly straight line. The map I have proves it. So you see, finally I shall reach the foundations of the tower. No other buildings will get in the way because the tunnel follows deep under the main road leading to the central square where the tower is situated—"

"Good Lord, if it were possible to get inside the tower—!" Ted broke in breathlessly.

"We might learn plenty," Cavil commented. "That will take time though—and I have so little time to spare. Nevertheless, it will be well worth the struggle. And here"—he swung round—"are my tools and apparatus."

He tapped various efficient though roughly designed machines affectionately, stooped and mused before a device resembling a radio-televizor.

"This may interest you," he remarked, looking up. "Just think of something, will you? Anything will do."

Ted nodded and thought rather bitterly of Madge. A switch on the machine clicked under the scientist's hand—then Ted stared in surprise as the screen of the apparatus gave a perfect picture of Madge just as he had envisioned her.

"What in hell—" he began in amazement, and with a chuckle Cavil switched the instrument off. "Thought reader," he smiled. "I've only had it finished a couple of days."

"If only we could get the apparatus near Madge!" Ted cried. "Think of it! Her every thought revealed—"

"I know…" Cavil frowned. "I'm working on that problem right now. The apparatus needs increasing in range: once I can do that I can reach her thoughts from this very spot. Trouble is, the whole apparatus is too heavy to move about, otherwise I could shorten the range a good deal by taking it down the tunnel."

He turned aside to a half assembled device of copper wire wound round drums, connected in turn to crystalline bars, insulation blocks, and glass tubes.

"The energy machine I told you about," he explained. "Three times more powerful than the Empress' device. You may be aware that her instruments generate a shield of energy, which sets molecules in vibration so that no ordinary power can break through them? Well, this is far more efficient. A shield generated from this energy could break down one of hers! Also you know that her beam works by shifting atoms out of their positions and causing disintegration? I can do better!

"My force causes molecules to polarize to any desired degree.

Each molecule is, as you may know, a tiny magnet with north and south poles. When the beam wave from this machine is generated it forces molecules to swing exactly as I wish.

"See the possibilities? I can either create matter so tough and compressed that nothing can shatter it, or else I can so alter and coordinate its molecules as to destroy all its original form and eliminate friction and cohesion. Result is total collapse of the matter concerned and its transformation into energy. That definitely goes one better than the Empress' subatomic device which merely displaces, but does not destroy matter."

The silence of speculation fell on them for a moment, then again Cavil became active. Opening a cupboard he produced picks and shovels, opened the heavy door and led the way with flashlight into the tunnel. Ted, pick and shovel under his arm, followed behind until they arrived at the rocky earth barring their path.

"Incidentally," Ted remarked, as Cavil put the lamp down, "where do you put the earth you dig out?"

"I wait until I have a good quantity then transport it back into the laboratory. After that it's a simple matter to carry it to one of the several disused sewer areas branching off the main one leading to the lab. Slow work, but it can't be helped. Once I've finished my energy machine the thing will be easy. The barrier will simply be converted into energy. Now, let's start. We've wasted enough time talking."

Ted nodded, tugged off his coat.

Suddenly, life was worth living again. He was working for a purpose—the unraveling of the mystery that clouded his whole existence, the mystery of why one girl had sacrificed her entire soul and decency on an altar of world power.

Savagely he dug his pick into the mass—again and again, watched powdered stone and rubbish fly in all directions.

"Not too fiercely!" Cavil warned him. "Though we're not likely to be heard we can't afford to take any chances."

Suddenly Ted gave a yelp as his pick rebounded with stinging force from something of almost incredible hardness. He nursed his palms and glared down at the rock, seized the flashlight and held it closer.

"Metal!" he exclaimed in surprise. "And that wallop I gave it hasn't even scratched it. If this goes for any distance we're going to have a swell time breaking through it."

He seized his pick again, hammered away the rock from around the small section of metal he had struck. Yet in every direction he and Cavil worked they struck more metal—until it became depressingly evident that the passage was blocked from side to side with a veritable wall of the stuff.

"Damn!" Cavil breathed fervently. "We must have struck the foundations of some old building."

He frowned, went on his knees and studied the metal closely, hammered his pick point against it. Not even a scratch resulted.

"Looks as if we'll have to detour somehow," he grunted; then for a long time he was silent, presently looked up. "I guess I don't know what sort of metal this is. It's tougher than either iron or steel—"

"Say!" Ted breathed, snapping his fingers suddenly.

"Well?" Cavil's white head jerked round. "What's wrong?"

"I've just thought of something. Just whereabouts are we at the moment? I mean in relation to old New York?"

Cavil tugged a soiled map out of his pocket and studied the penciled lines that indicated his tunnel. After some study he said:

"About three feet or so from the site of the old Museum of Natural History, shelled to pieces during the war. Why?"

"It's a cinch!" Ted breathed, his eyes gleaming. "Remember that meteorite you visited at Pottstown?"

"Naturally. What about it?"

"It was removed to the Museum," Ted went on eagerly. "What would happen during a bombardment? The thing was so tough nothing could make an impression on it; a million to one it would sink down through the shattered floor and become buried in debris. I'll stake my whole life on the fact that this darned metal here is that meteorite itself—unbreakable, impregnable. If I'm right we'll never get through it, unless of course we make a detour."

"You are right, must be," Cavil answered slowly, thinking. "The coincidence is too obvious to be missed. But I don't altogether agree that it means a detour. My energy projector will go through it; no matter ever created can stop it—"

He looked up with keen eyes. "That's our next course, Ted. Finish the projector before anything else—then we'll blast through the tunnel and this stuff as well—right onwards to the tower. Now let's get back to the lab."

They turned and headed back up the tunnel. Once more in the laboratory they plunged into a frenzy of activity on the half finished projector. Ted, knowing nothing of the workings, could only do as the scientist ordered, and he found the work fascinating enough. Hour by hour they worked on.

The small hours had arrived before they sneaked back from their underground hideout to the billet to secure a much needed sleep.

CHAPTER VI

A Tremendous Discovery

The following day Ted received his first initiation into the grueling labor of machine minder in the Extraction Plant. He spent twelve grinding hours—excepting for meal intervals—before a whirring, complex machine.

In the great throbbing hall of industry he saw the transparent tubes which brought the pumped chlorophyll from the vegetated areas of the country, saw the alcohol compression machines by which the chlorophyll was refined to deep green solution and run off into vats traveling on an endless conveyor belt—thence to parts unknown, presumably for sealing in the cylinders.

The whole setup fascinated him by its very mystery. The testing chambers, too, were masterpieces of efficiency, wherein robot control tested the spectrum of the refined chlorophyll, its purity being decided by its absorption bands in the red and orange regions.

Strange, Ted reflected, that the girl should have such far-reaching knowledge. Everything on every hand bespoke a brain of a power which, to be absolutely truthful, he had never thought the girl had possessed..

How many thousands of gallons of chlorophyll passed through his own particular machine unit during the day he could not imagine; it all left him with the grim fear that this was driving Nature too far. The stuff was patently being extracted far faster than it could ever be replaced, hastening on all too obvious doom of the Earth itself.

And yet why? What had Madge Cromwell to gain by ruining the very world she had conquered? That was where the mystery lay.

In the evening Ted forgot most of his fears in returning to the underground laboratory with Cavil.

But they worked for several weeks, a little at a time, before the old scientist was finally satisfied—weeks in which the flow of chlorophyll had gone on, weeks in which Ted had seen, on one occasion, some five hundred tightly sealed cylinders, with detonators on their ends, fired into space from a solitary cannon pit just outside New York. Whither the cylinders went upon leaving the Earth nobody knew—except Madge Cromwell. That very thought made his urge to finish the tower tunnel all the mightier.

And now Cavil had the instrument finished, fingered its queer outlines gently. He surveyed the neat storage batteries attached to it, by which means, so long as the charge lasted, it was entirely portable and self-contained.

"Now to see what happens!" he said anxiously. "I've fixed a resistance so the strength can be built up gradually. Also I have incorporated a shutter to narrow the width of the beam."

Picking the instrument up in his arms he led the way into the tunnel, set the machine down a couple of feet from the metal barrier.

Ted held the torch, watched as the scientist carefully moved his switches. Instantly a hardly visible pencil of deep red light sprang from the projecting lens of the apparatus, struck clean in the center of the metal and rock crusted wall.

The result was amazing. The encompassed point flowed and dissolved within itself, soundlessly but inevitably. A weird streaming flux grew larger and larger as matter everywhere in that circumscribed area ceased to be, changed itself into energy that made the skin of the two men tingle and set their hair nearly standing on end. Their eyes smarted with invisible radiations. The whole atmosphere around them was suddenly alive with static forces.

"Better wear these," Cavil said briefly, and tugged specially made goggles out of his pocket, handed a pair to Ted. Then, the strain on their eyes relieved, they returned to watch that flaming core of power.

Within minutes, or so it seemed, the beam had sunk clean

through the barrier.

"Then it is hollow," Cavil murmured. "I suspected it. Its weight on being removed to the museum was entirely disproportionate to its size, and such dense metal too."

He shifted the projector a little, cut a flowing, sweeping circle and finally had an opening large enough to permit entrance. Then he stopped the power and taking the torch he began to scramble through the hole he had made. Ted followed after him, discovered that the meteorite was indeed hollow, with a wall two feet thick. Two feet of un-scratchable metal vaporized in twenty minutes! It enlisted within him a new respect for Cavil's genius.

To his surprise, on emerging from the hole he discovered not an empty hole with a wall beyond it—but a small area of machinery hemmed in by smooth, curved walls! In the center of this stood Cavil, gazing round in bewilderment on multiple switches, charts, a chair bolted to the metal floor, reflecting prisms.

He wheeled suddenly, crossed over to a barely perceptible line in the smooth metal, which indicated a door. Silently he studied it.

"Good—Heavens!" he breathed incredulously. "Ted, do you realize what this meteor is? It's a space machine, composed of immensely tough metal to stand the impact of atmospheric friction and the meteoroids and brickbats of empty space. Look around you! What is more, this door is so devised that it opens only by a combination lock, either from inside or outside."

"But—but where the devil did it come from?" Ted demanded, gazing round. "And if it comes to that, why?"

"I don't know—yet." Cavil was so eager he had become impatient. He went round the small space like a bloodhound, staring at the machinery, probing his torch beam into every corner, peering at the controls. Ted nosed around too, but found little to explain the mystery. Then suddenly Cavil called him.

"Take a look at this chart!"

Ted obeyed, but to his non-astronomical mind it conveyed little—was composed of lines, both straight and wavy ones, drawn from one circle to another, with several other circles of varying sizes lying in different directions.

"I don't get it," he frowned. "Maybe I'm dumb—"

"Definitely!" Cavil growled. He jabbed his finger on the chart.

"This big central circle is the sun. The two circles on the top left represent our nearest stellar neighbours: the double suns of Alpha and Proxima Centauri. Now, these lines here are drawn from Alpha Cebtauri—obviously by somebody with an extremely good knowledge of space drifts, gravity fields, and so forth. In other words, a first class interstellar scientist. All the lines converge on one point—the third circle from the sun. That's Earth, of course."

"You—you mean this thing came from Alpha Centauri?" Ted gasped blankly.

"The thing's obvious—but don't ask me the reason it happened. Somebody drove it here! The only explanation I can think of is that the person or being remained inside here until this 'meteorite' was taken to the Museum. Then simply walked out."

"But the person from Alpha Centauri," Ted persisted. "What happened to him? Damn it all, any kid knows that no two beings of different worlds can be exactly alike. An alien being would be instantly discovered."

"Yes, I suppose so." Cavil stood in deep thought for several minutes, then he said, "That part puzzles roe plenty. We do know that an alien is somewhere on Earth—and that ever since this meteorite fell strange things have been happening, in which Madge Crormwell, daughter of the world's former greatest scientist, is deeply involved. Where exactly does she fit into the puzzle?"

"Suppose," said Ted slowly, "that the alien is in hiding—or even can make himself invisible—and is hypnotizing Madge for his own purposes? That she isn't the master of her own wm?"

Cavil looked at Ted thoughtfully. "Have you seen her face to face since she became Empress?"

"Sure."

"So have I—and did she strike you as being hypnotized? No, Ted. I never saw a girl so completely in possession of her faculties. That's the problem. The only way to really discover is by my mind reader."

Cavil paused and surveyed Ted steadily.

"Listen, Ted," he said quietly, "this new revelation puts a very different face on things. We're fighting the ingenuity of people of another world. For some reason they are deliberately stealing chlorophyll from Earth. Whether or not the chlorophyll is destined for

Alpha Centauri we don't know—but Madge Cromwell's mind will tell us. We've got to work fast from now on, stop this dangerous scheme before it gets any further. We'll have to divide our labors. You continue digging the tunnel by means of the projector, blast out the other side of this space meteorite and go forward through the tunnel's continuation. For my part I'll bend all my energies to enlarging the range of my thought reader. Can't bring it down here, unfortunately; it's a fixture. That's our next course. Now you carry on; I'm going back to the laboratory."

* * * *

And from that moment they started on their divergent paths, working night after night. During the ordinary day work they heard the first alarming reports from different parts of the world concerning the effect of the chlorophyll draining.

Two things were happening. Vegetation of course died with its essential constituent removed—or else became a weakly, faded version of its natural self. This very fact, in America and England at least, was producing disastrous effects on the staple food trade. Animals were running short of food; frantic bargaining had begun; prices were soaring. But the relentless extraction of chlorophyll went on and all deputations to Madge Cromwell to stop this slow killing of a world were met with flat refusals.

There was a bigger, graver danger, too. The atmosphere was slowly becoming vitiated. It would be many months, even perhaps some years, before it became rankly poisonous—but definitely such a thing would come to pass if matters went unchecked. The essential task of chlorophyll to break down carbon dioxide and release oxygen under the stimulus of sunlight was being gradually stopped. In the end it could only mean that the air itself would get overburdened with a preponderance of toxic air, and the consequent asphyxiation of all living things.

Yet mankind dared not rebel. So far as humanity knew, the woman in the tower still held the whip hand. Week after week the work went on; week after week the endless numbers of chlorophyll-filled cylinders were fired into space.

And down in the underground laboratory Justin Cavil and Ted worked onwards with steady persistency. Ted in fact had driven the tunnel to within a few feet of the foundation walls of the tower. There he stopped, afraid to venture further without the scientist's further instructions—but as yet Cavil was too busy otherwise to give the matter his attention.

His whole being was absorbed in the task of putting the finishing touches to a range-widening device for his mind-reader, a feat which he finally accomplished by stepping up the power and consequent area of reception. So, little by little, using a little more power each time, incorporating fresh turns on his coils, removing others, he achieved the necessary balance, found the exact area in space in which the girl herself invariably moved—the controlling office of the tower.

For three nights the two men labored to bring her thoughts to their screen, but failed owing to her absence from headquarters. On the fourth night, however, there was a change. Images began to come through, crowded onto the screen.

Both men sat in breathless intensity, watching the swirling visions forming before them.

It was a vision of machinery, which just as quickly merged into a clear cut cameo of a hideous looking object not unlike a mammoth scorpion, its gigantic eyes staring, with horrible intensity into a massive drum-like object banked with tubes.

"A—an Alphan?" suggested Ted, horrified, and Cavil nodded slowly.

"Possibly. Evidently the Empress is thinking about Alpha Centauri."

"But how can she?" Ted demanded, bewildered. "She's never been there; doesn't know anything about it. Unless it's really hypnotism. In which case she would only see what the mind in control wishes her to see."

"Actually it definitely disproves hypnotism," Cavil answered slowly. "If it were hypnotism this machine would not work because it is attuned to her brain, not to the emanations of the brain in control. There'd be just a blank. No, these are her actual thoughts, but how she— Look!" he finished quickly.

The view had changed now, was encompassing a vision of New York.

With the natural rapidity of thought itself, as the impressions drifted through the girl's keen brain--—whether actual observations or merely memory impressions—the views dissolved into one another and had real sense and continuity only to their owner.

With surprising swiftness New York dissolved into a cannon pit, from which vomited countless hundreds of chlorophyll shells. A momentary glimpse of infinite space, then a fetid, steamy wilderness drifted into view, in which no thing stirred as yet, but where entire areas were smothered in monstrous green splotches, There was a series of explosions, which could only mean the arrival of a number of chlorophyll shells.

"Great Heavens, it's Venus!" gasped Cavil, turning an amazed face to stare at Ted. "It can't be anywhere else! The outer planets are too far away to be reached by cannon, even with atomic force. Mars is dead, Mercury is airless and alternatively frozen and scorched. That leaves only Venus. What the devil does it all mean, I wonder? Hello, what's this?"

The scene was not very startling, merely back to New York again and the headquarters office itself—but now it had come to actual perception—instead of what had clearly been either memory or imagination—there was something odd about the picture. It was blurred, split up in the queerest fashion; actually some kind of superimposition with one view overlying the other.

As far as the straining men could make out, a laboratory was overlying the view of an old man, and the old man was the dead Asa Cromwell himself, staring dumbfounded in front of him— Then the scene swamped itself with a picture of New York. It broke up into weird double sections—New York, Ted himself, Asa Cromwell, hurtling meteor, Alpha Centauri, Venus—all interwoven in a mad complex.

"This is impossible!" gasped Cavil amazedly. "No mind, however great, can think of two things at one and the same time. And yet here we have it. It must be her brain because no other could be identical. That means—"

"Wait!" Ted cried, leaping up wildly. "Wait a minute! I believe I've got it! Anyway, it's worth risking. Madge is in the tower now and the rest of the place will be pretty well deserted for the night. We're going to blast the remaining few feet of tunnel and get inside— It's a cinch to catch her alone. Even if we don't that energy gun will take care of everything. Now come on."

"But—but why?" Cavil gasped blankly. "We haven't—"

"Don't argue!" Ted yelled. "I've got the solution! Hurry up!"

CHAPTER VII

The Alphan

It was only a matter of minutes to gain the remaining barrier in the tunnel. Ted didn't stop for anything, not even to speak. He went to work with a grim determination that had the old scientist utterly baffled.

He watched in silence as Ted drove the energy pencil into the remaining rock and metal foundations. In less than fifteen minutes he had made a hole large enough to scramble through into the lowest basement of the tower itself.

There was nobody in sight. The torch beam traveled over endless neatly stacked cases, all the paraphernalia of a basement warehouse.

"O. K.," Ted whispered. "We're going up to Madge's office if we have to blast our way there. I'm asking no questions of anybody. If they try to stop us—" and he patted the energy gun apparatus significantly.

Though he could not entirely understand the urgency Cavil cooperated willingly enough. The storeroom door was their first barrier, until the lock vaporized under the gun. Then the path was easier.

By slow degrees they worked their way up the cavernous staircase to the lower floors—the offices, checking rooms, anterooms.

Suddenly a dim form loomed up before them, and behind him another. Guards! Ted swung the energy pencil up and it flicked once, twice. With a moan the first man sank to the floor, acrid flesh odors in the air as smoke rose from his breast. The other staggered, and a moan of intense pain escaped his lips.

Leaping forward, Ted swung a heavy fist against the man's jaw and knocked him unconscious.

"Poor fellow," he muttered. "Had to do it, both to keep him from spreading the alarm, and from suffering the pain of that energy burn. We'll have to come back and take care of him…if we succeed in what we are doing."

They went on now, and a few floors further up, shrank against a wall, as another watchman walked slowly past a divergent corridor, unaware of their presence.

Up and up to the topmost floor of all, region of the girl's own dreaded power. A single light glowed on the corridor outside her office.

"Leave all the talking to me," Ted whispered, his face grimly set. Then grasping the door handle of the office he pushed gently. It was not locked. It swung wide, framed him on the threshold.

The great office beyond was mainly in shadow. The main lights were off; a single desk lamp cast a circle of brilliance on Madge Cromwell's dark, shining head—then suddenly it changed to her face as she looked up in surprise at the deeply shadowed form regarding her.

"Who is it?" she demanded shortly. "What do you want?"

Ted eyed her, smiling twistedly. "Lock the door, Cavil," he commanded coldly; then he moved forward slowly until he and the girl were facing each other across the desk. Her face was rigid, hard, her eyes bitter pools of darkness. Abruptly the lights came up as Cavil found the switch, turned the girl's face to a dead white mask.

"So it's you, Ted," she said slowly—then sharply, "What do you want? How did you get in here?"

He still stood staring at her with smoldering, malevolent eyes.

"Well, well, speak!" she burst out fiercely. "Say something!"

"I will…" His voice was amazingly steady, had in it all the depths of bitterness. He moved forward a little, rested his elbows on the desk and stared the girl full in the eyes. Under his elbows he felt switches grind.

Then suddenly springing forward he clutched the girl by the throat, heaved, dragged her by main strength clean across the desk and hurled her, sprawling and dazed, to the carpet.

"You devil! You consummate she-devil!" he breathed in cold fury. "Of course you showed no mercy! Of course you didn't, damn you, because you had no reason to!"

"Take it easy, Ted," Cavil put in anxiously.

"Easy!" he bellowed. "Good God, man, don't you realize that

it's our turn now—? Get up, you!" he roared demoniacally, and suddenly thrusting his hands under the startled girl's armpits he swept her up from the floor, raised her until her alarmed face was within inches of his own. There he held her by main strength, her feet kicking in furious helplessness against his legs.

"Now get this," he whispered. "I know your secret—I know all about you! I'm trying to remember that you're a woman—at least I suppose you are—but so help me, if you don't spill the whole story I'll kill you—little by little, break every bone in your body one by one. It's up to you," he finished significantly, then suddenly lowering to the floor he gave her a shove that sent her reeling into a chair, shaken and dazed.

In a moment his powerful hands had clamped her wrists tightly to the chair arms.

"Well?" he asked sardonically, and there was no mercy in his face.

"I—I don't know what you're talking about!" she panted thickly. "You can't do this to me! I'll—"

"Oh, no, you won't," Ted broke in shortly, and he suddenly transferred his hands to entirely encircle her wrists, began to turn them slowly. The girl's face whitened; her teeth began to dig into her lower lip.

"Remember," he grated out, "I can do this longer than you can stand it. And I won't let up until you speak. Now, talk!"

He went on twisting slowly and relentlessly until the girl began to squirm under the pain.

"I—I don't know what you mean," she gasped hoarsely. "I'll have you killed for this! I—Ohh!" She broke off with a scream as the grip became more vicious and her shoulder twisted.

"Ted, you can't do this to the girl you really love!" Cavil gasped in horror. "Stop it, you madman—"

"It so happens that this isn't the girl I really love!" Ted replied stonily. "Is it?" he demanded, glaring into the girl's furious, pain ridden face. *"You are not Madge Cromwell!"* he roared. "Admit it, damn you—admit it!"

"What?" gasped Cavil in consternation. *"Not* Madge Cromwell—? But she must be! She—"

"A perfect image of her, but not the real Madge!" Ted ground out. "Confess it—!" He gave the girl's arms a final wrench then disgustedly hurled her out of the chair to the floor. She lay there, rubbing her tortured arms.

"She isn't Madge," Ted repeated, striding round her and glaring down on her. "Your mind reader, Cavil, showed that two minds were on the same wavelength—two brains, identical, thinking different thoughts at the same time. Two editions of the same brain. Two Madge Cromwells! The real Madge is the one who called me on the telephone so long ago, the one I briefly saw in the elevator more recently. Remember me telling you about the ultra violet photo she took of her dead father's retinae? The girl in that picture was this Madge here—the one who killed Cromwell. The real Madge thought her father caught a glimpse of her before he died. He did not. The woman he saw was this fiend. Am I right?" he demanded, glowering down.

"You driveling fool!" the girl on the floor retorted, glaring up. "I tell you I'm Madge Cromwell and you'll suffer for this! I'll have you—"

"Right, you've asked for it!" Ted barked suddenly. "I've no compunction regarding what I do to you. I'll learn the truth even if I have to murder you!"

"Try it!" she retorted defiantly.

For answer he swept her threshing body into his arms, flung her in her office chair and tied her down with his belt. Then, though it went somewhat against the grain, he put into force a devilish routine of third degree. Switching off the main lights he trained the blazing desk light directly on the girl' face, hammered her with questions, used every means of subtle torture he could devise.

An hour crawled by and the stubborn dark head still shook. Another half hour—then at last the terrific strain snapped even her iron reserve. She broke down with a sobbing gasp of exhaustion.

"All right—all right, it's true," she gulped. "I'm not Madge Cromwell. I'm—I'm from a world circling the star you call Alpha Centauri. I'm an Alphan, patterned in form exactly like Madge Cromwell.

"My race have studied your solar system, and Earth in particular, for many years. First, we sent robot probes. Landing unobserved on your moon, they studied your planet telescopically, and monitored your broadcasts, transmitting the data back to my home planet.

"We decided to send an advance party, of which I was a member. Our spaceship took several years to reach your system, during which time we slept in suspended animation.

"Eventually reaching the outskirts of your system, we were revived. To escape detection from Earth, our spaceship landed on the far side of your moon, just beyond the terminator line.

"My people sent me as their agent. Our plans had been well laid. Having studied Earth for years, we saw how, without endangering ourselves or giving anything away, we could master this world and use its most valuable constituent—chlorphyll—for our own purposes. For the execution of this plan we needed great manpower—more than we have got—and also somebody on Earth with weapons so powerful nobody could stand against them. Our own are too heavy for transport."

The girl paused, gasping heavily from her ordeal.

"Our telescopic devices finally discovered Asa Cromwell, and for several years followed his activities, and those of his daughter. The old man was too difficult to duplicate, nor would the reason have been so convincing. Better to use his daughter, who might conceivably be young and foolish enough to get ideas about world power and go crazy with her father's discoveries.

"His daughter was studied by our medical experts, both externally and internally by telescopic X-rays. Her every organ was duplicated, her every scar and mark, down to the last hair on her head. I was the subject, underwent the painful process of re-patterning by slow degrees. Months of hell, which made me the image of her.

"So I came to Earth…"

The Alphan woman paused again tossed damp black hair from her face.

"I came in what you thought was a meteor. When it was put in the Museum I easily escaped. I could talk your language easily because years of monitoring your radio and television has taught my people the syllables peculiar to this country. It was simple on arrival to track down Asa Cromwell in his laboratory. I had only to await a time when his place was free for a while of protective forces, step in as his daughter, and kill him.

"We had a fight when it came to the final issue, knocked over several instruments—then I believe the knowledge of being slain by his own daughter was too much for him—and he died. It saved me the trouble of using more obvious methods."

"Well?" Ted ground out. "What else?"

"Later I went to New York, walked in on Madge Cromwell. I had, of course kept careful watch over her movements. The hotel had no thoughts other than that I was the same Madge Cromwell who had signed the register. My clothes were identical, and certainly my face and figure were. So I took Madge Cromwell away in one of her own trunks. Once she broke away and rang you up. I stunned her—but I let you come in order to be rid of you finally and completely."

"Since you killed Asa Cromwell, why not her?" Cavil demanded.

"Is it not obvious?" the alien woman asked coldly. "When my work is finished on this world I intend to leave her in my place to take the entire blame. In that way nobody will ever know the truth. Though she will tell the story, who will believe?"

"But—but *why* all this elaborate preparation, this perfect cover up?" Ted cried. "I can understand you leaving Madge to take the rap, and thereby leaving yourselves free from any chance of vengeance in the future—but why the struggle anyhow?"

"It's a plain story of necessity," the girl answered. "Our world is practically exhausted of its natural resources. Venus is the best possible next planet for us because of its nearness to the sun, similar to the position occupied by my home world. In our natural form we thrive on great heat, I of course have sacrificed my birthright for my people. Venus has an atmosphere in which oxygen is absent—therefore as it stands the planet is no use to us. To generate enough oxygen for the whole of Venus would be impossible—hence our idea of using chlorphyll, in which Earth abounds. Used in combination with specially bred bacteria. The chlorophyll will create oxygen in the Venusian atmosphere, forming starch in the process of photosynthesis, utilizing the energy of sunlight and liberating oxygen in the process. It will make vast changes on Venus in a very short space of time, and gradually the planet will develop a breathable atmosphere.

"Very soon now we will send a radio message to our home

world, and their exodus to this system can begin. It will take our message years to reach them, of course, and more years for their journey here. But by that time Venus will become a planet suitable for us. Earth will have died, no doubt, for the amount of chlorophyll we will need, in order to speed up the bacterial process as quickly as possible, will drain Earth entirely. Not that it matters. The people of Earth are an extremely stupid race at the best. The chlorophyll and bacteria containers are fired with detonators so that they will explode on landing. Already, even if I were to fail now, my work is done. Breathable air has come to Venus. But I must go on and on.

"Now you know," she finished slowly. "Nov you know why I have invented things rather surprising in the matter of machinery— why I linked atomic power to a stolen airplane at the outset of my conquest. Manpower was needed and a world rich in chlorophyll. What better world than Earth? A desperate race will take desperate measures— Like me!" she wound up savagely, and her hands, which had been hidden in the shadow under the desk suddenly rose up, holding something glittering. A drawer lay open—

Instinctively Ted and Cavil fell to one side, just in time to see a savage beam of energy slice a piece out of the wall nearby. Before they could fully grasp the situation the girl had severed the belt that held her body, leaped to her feet.

"As I said, my plan will go on," she muttered venomously. "Do you think for one moment that I would let you get away with all you now know? Oh—no!" She leveled her gun steadily and the two men looked helplessly towards their distant force gun projector. She smiled icily.

"I'm going to kill you," she explained smoothly. "You have tortured me, forced the truth out of me—but it will do you no good."

She raised the gun a little and Ted waited bitterly for the end, Cavil beside him.

But the end did not come. Instead there was a sudden explosion from the window to the rear of them—a tinkling of glass. The girl looked up in sudden alarm, and in that second red suddenly stained the whiteness of her breast above the heart.

The gun dropped out of her hand, her face contorted. With a little moan she fell back helplessly in her chair, hands pressed to the wound.

Ted had hardly recovered from his surprise before a splintering of further glass arrested his attention. A man vaulted into the room, revolver in hand, leapt swiftly across to the door and unlocked it. It vomited a struggling, shouting mob of people.

"What the devil—" Ted began in bewilderment; then he swung round as the man with the revolver drew from the crowd and came quickly forward.

"Tell you in a minute," he panted. "Look...!"

The crowd had halted before the woman in the chair. For a moment her dimmed dark eyes looked across at Ted.

"Per—perhaps it doesn't matter," she said in a low voice. "I've started—started the new world for my people. You—you still have your world." She gave a twisted, sardonic smile. "I shan't need to— to build a space ship to return to my people after all—"

Her eyes closed slowly; her head dropped forward. For a moment the angry crowd stood silent, then with a roar they swept in on upon her, raised her high over their heads and bore her to the window. With terrific force they hurled her body against the already broken glass, watched it go hurtling down into the yawning dark.

Cold wind blew in from the window. Sobered, the people turned, grim faced and flushed with vengeful satisfaction.

"You see," said the man with the gun, turning, "we heard her entire confession. I'm one of her night watchmen. Somehow the microphone in this room, connecting with the rest of the building got into contact. Anyhow, there I was down below, marching around, when all of a sudden I started to hear everything going on in here. I called the people in from outside to listen. On every floor the confession could be heard. I couldn't hold them; they were mad with lynch lust.

"We came up here and the door was locked. I went along the parapet to this window and saw what was happening through the chink in the curtains. I'm darned glad it was my hand that finally killed that she-devil from Alpha. My wife and kids died because of her!"

There came growls of assent from the mob. Still others were pressing in from the corridor.

"It must have been my leaning on the desk that livened the

mike," Ted panted. "I remember now—I did feel switches under my elbow— Thank Heaven her confession was heard; Madge would never have been believed otherwise. But where is she?" he went on desperately, twirling round. "The woman said something about a basement—"

"Guess I know," one of the men said. "There's a passage near one of the basements that's always kept locked. I've had to guard it without knowing what's been on the other side. Elevator is the only direct contact with it. I was always sent away when the door of the place was opened— But we don't know the combination of the lock," he finished uncertainly. "She knew that."

Ted glanced towards the energy projector. "Let's go!" he said curtly.

In five minutes the private elevator had dropped to the lowest levels, faced a small square of corridor and a heavy steel door.

"Hey, there! Madge!" Ted bawled, but there was no response.

"Guess the door's soundproof," said the man who had been the guard. "I've never heard a sound from inside."

Ted nodded grimly, switched on the projector and burned steadily on the lock. When he had driven a small hole through the door there came a cry from beyond.

"Who's there? What's happening?"

"Madge!" Ted yelped in hysterical delight. "Hang on!"

He burned away again with savage fury until at last the entire lock had vaporized. The crowd pushed the door open. Beyond was a fairly comfortable cell, dimly lit. Madge Cromwell herself, so staggeringly like her dead image that even Ted was bewildered for a moment, was seated on the bed, a gown thrown hastily around her.

She came forward slowly—then as she spoke Ted's last trace of bafflement went. That same quiet voice, that same sweet expression.

"Oh, Ted… Thank God! That awful creature—"

She gulped helplessly, burst into a flood of tears.

"There now, forget it," Ted murmured gently, pillowing her dark head on his shoulder. "It's finished with. She's dead, and you are free. And there'll never be a next time. The world goes on—a changed world—learned a lot by experience and only just escaped its doom. But you're the same old Madge and I'm just the same old

Ted, I guess. Eh, Cavil?"

The scientist smiled, said nothing.

ABOUT THE AUTHOR

British writer **JOHN RUSSELL FEARN** was born near Manchester, England, in 1908. As a child he devoured the science fiction of Wells and Verne, and was a voracious reader of the Boys' Story Papers. He was also fascinated by the cinema, and first broke into print in 1931 with a series of articles in *Film Weekly*.

He then quickly sold his first novel, *The Intelligence Gigantic*, to the American magazine, *Amazing Stories*. Over the next fifteen years, writing under several pseudonyms, Fearn became one of the most prolific contributors to all of the leading US science fiction pulps, including such legendary publications as *Astounding Stories*, *Startling Stories*, *Thrilling Wonder Stories*, and *Weird Tales*.

During the late 1940s he diversified into writing novels for the UK market, and also created his famous superwoman character, The Golden Amazon, for the prestigious Canadian magazine, the Toronto *Star Weekly*. In the early 1950s in the UK, his fifty-two novels as "Vargo Statten" were bestsellers, most notably his novelization of the film, *Creature from the Black Lagoon*.

Apart from science fiction, he had equal success with westerns, romances, and detective fiction, writing an amazing total of 180 novels—most of them in a period of just ten years—before his early death in 1960. His work has been translated into nine languages, and continues to be reprinted and read worldwide.

MORE BORGO PRESS TITLES
BY JOHN RUSSELL FEARN

THE ADAM QUIRK SERIES

The Master Must Die: A Science Fiction Mystery
The Lonely Astronomer : A Science Fiction Mystery

THE ANJANI SERIES

The Gold of Akada: A Jungle Adventure Novel
Anjani the Mighty: A Lost Race Novel

THE BLACK MARIA SERIES

Black Maria, M.A.: A Classic Crime Novel
The Murdered Schoolgirl: A Classic Crime Novel
One Remained Seated: A Classic Crime Novel
Thy Arm Alone: A Classic Crime Novel
Death in Silhouette: A Classic Crime Novel

THE HERBERT THE DINOSAUR SERIES

A Thing of the Past
The Genial Dinosaur

OTHER BOOKS

1,000-Year Voyage: A Science Fiction Novel
Account Settled: A Science Fiction Mystery

Before Earth Came: Classic Science Fiction Stories
Bury the Hatchet: A Crime Tale
A Case for Brutus Lloyd: A Science Fiction Mystery
The Crimson Rambler: A Crime Novel
Don't Touch Me: A Crime Novel
Dynasty of the Small: Classic Science Fiction Stories
The Empty Coffins: A Mystery of Horror
The Fourth Door: A Mystery Novel
From Afar: A Science Fiction Mystery
Fugitive of Time: A Classic Science Fiction Novel
The G-Bomb: A Science Fiction Novel
The Haunted Gallery: Crime Stories
Here and Now: A Science Fiction Novel
Into the Unknown: A Science Fiction Tale
Last Conflict: Classic Science Fiction Stories
Legacy from Sirius: A Classic Science Fiction Novel
The Man from Hell: Classic Science Fiction Stories
The Man Who Was Not: A Crime Novel
Manton's World: A Classic Science Fiction Novel
Moon Magic: A Novel of Romance (as Elizabeth Rutland)
One Way Out: A Crime Novel (with Philip Harbottle)
Pattern of Murder: A Classic Crime Novel
Reflected Glory: A Dr. Castle Classic Crime Novel
Robbery Without Violence: Two Science Fiction Crime Stories
Rule of the Brains: Classic Science Fiction Stories
Shattering Glass: A Crime Novel
The Silvered Cage: A Scientific Murder Mystery
Slaves of Ijax: A Science Fiction Novel
Something from Mercury: Classic Science Fiction Stories
The Space Warp: A Science Fiction Novel
The Time Trap: A Science Fiction Novel
Valley of Pretenders: Classic Science Fiction Stories
Vision Sinister: A Scientific Detective Thriller
Voice of the Conqueror: A Classic Science Fiction Novel
What Happened to Hammond? A Scientific Mystery
Within That Room!: A Classic Crime Novel
World Without Chance: Classic Science Fiction Stories